I0545585

# Tehachapi

### Book Two
### Duke and Angela Series

# Brent Carr

**BETHANY PUBLISHING GROUP**

1603 Capitol Ave.,

Cheyenne, WY 82001

This is Book 2 of the Duke and Angela series.

Brent Carr,

TEHACHAPI

ISBN-13: 978-1-939395-04-7

ISBN-10: 1939395046

This is a work of fiction. Names, character, incidents are the product of the author's imagination or used fictitiously, and any resemblance to actual persons, living or dead, businesses, companies, events or locales are incidental.

DEDICATION

To Cory and Andrew—my sons.

# Chapter 1

**Too Little, Too Slow.** I think my first memory was last night, shortly before dawn. Perhaps, it was the piercing cold — my bones ached as if I lived in the artic. Or else, the remembrance formed as the water ran down my nose, and a stalactite grew.

Protruding downward from my nose, the ice was about an inch and a half long.

"The frigid gust of wind blazing down from the mountains helped form my first recorded thought," I said to myself.

Frankly, I do not know why I cannot remember things from before. Those around me, who are roughly the same ages, delight in telling tales. Possibly, my earlier memories are all too painful.

It's now six a.m. or shortly thereafter. The sun is starting to peak above the ridges of the tree-lined mountains. Still too early for the light to bring any relief from the cold that strangles me. Feels as if every step, I take drives a nail into the tiny hips. My knees creak, and feet feel frozen.

My peers are running around in delight—freed to play outside. They seem oblivious to the inclement weather.

One of the half-brothers has told me how much he enjoys kicking at the snow.

I have to admit as I gaze east the new morning light is a spectacular sight — the spectacular creeps into Cummings Valley. We are only a tad above the five thousand-foot level; the air is pristine. I am now trying to jog a little, because my mom is getting on my back about loafing. She does not want me merely standing while everyone else frolics. Candidly, this so-called good life sucks. That fresh air hurts my lungs because it's so arctic.

"This is nothing – a day for sunbathing compared to Kentucky," my mom is telling me. "I remember when the snow was so bad that we couldn't even walk through the white, sticky goo to get back to the barn." She tells me her snow stories with pride.

I hate to be a whiner, who is always crabbing. The doctor says I was born premature, and I have significant 'birthing' problems. What does that mean, anyway? I don't know remember my birth either. All I grasp is I hurt with movement. I can't wait for summer.

"We've all told the stories of walking five miles uphill to the play yard, and then having to walk another five miles uphill back home," my mom jokes. "Here in Cummings Valley, your lungs get a chance to expand, and the days are truly God's miracle."

Finally, it is time for breakfast, which I admit is gamungus. Great — better than outstanding. Major league. Breakfast is the best part of the day.

Another problem I endure is most of my siblings are much bigger and stronger; and they push me out of the way when I come to getting at first pickings.

However, when it comes to eating, I am not shy, so I get my fair share. The doctor says I am scrawny. I need to eat more to grow up strong.

"You're such a little runt, honey. You must eat everything you can," says mom.

Rainy, who is the largest in our play yard, picks on me: "Pee-wee, get your butt out of my way, or I will crush you like a bug." He weighs about twice what I do. So, I'm sure he could make good on his promise.

Now with breakfast over, we always take time for some races. There are twelve of us in the fenced area, who compete against each other. To put it mildly, I have never come close to winning one of the speed-events. Today, I have a plan. I have snuck off halfway across the two hundred-yard pen. Mom sees I have skated out the lead.

"Ready set go," she yells.

"No problem," says Rainy.

The morn has warmed a bit. My joints are limbering up, and now that I have such an enormous lead; I feel confident about the situation. I kick up my heels and take off toward the other end.

"I've got you!" yells Rainy. He is fast – so big and so fast.

"Me too," says another.

"All of us," says Bart.

"Not this time," I cry. I am giving every ounce of energy. "You're not going to catch me this time."

"You lose," says Rainy, as he sprints by me with ease. He caught me with 30 yards to go.

"Me too," says Bart.

In the end, I have lost, horribly again. Eleven passed me, and are now making fun. I must admit several others who beat me could not be a snail.

They marched off to play with each other, and leave me "alone," like all the other losers from the ages past.

My mother makes her way over to me and explains, "We all grow at our own pace."

Not much comfort, mother, I say to myself.

"I can't even beat the smallest girl."

"Watch out," mom says, "that is sexist.  Many girls can out-run guys."

# Chapter 2

**The Warmth of a Friend**.  The day turns around when my sole friend, Nina Torres, comes to play.  Nina is seven years old.  She is the daughter of the farm manager Marty Torres.  Nina has long, curly, dark-brown hair with the biggest brown eyes. Gigantic.

My eyes are a shade of brown; hers are much browner.  Big – they are so large.

Doesn't really matter whether it's a bright sunny day; rainy or snowing.  Nina always comes.  She has the brightest smile and cheerful little voice.  My Nina is perfect.

Her brother Tommy, who is three years older, makes fun of Nina — because she moves with a noticeable limp.  He calls her "brace-leg."  Once Tommy's dad heard him, and gave him a licking.  The momentary brutality of father against his son has not changed a thing.  After the whipping, Nina's father gathered Tommy to him with a hug.  A telling sign of love.  We are the outcasts, and Tommy does not forget to remind us.

Nina cannot keep up with her dad or Tommy, because she walks so slowly.  She tracks behind.  Like me, she is left out.

As I say, "Nina is perfect."

We live on Dovato Farms in Tehachapi, California.  Tyler and Catrina Dovato are Bazsillionaires, who won the Kentucky Derby and the Breeders Cup numerous times.  They have ranches in Paso Robles, Kentucky and here in the Cummings Valley. Ours is a stone throw outside of the town of Tehachapi — two hours from LA.  We are the worst of their breeding farms, and no one fails to mention that fact either.

"Nina, how are you doing?"

"I'm great. You are walking much like me — with a limp. Was it cold last night?"

"Nina, you can't even imagine how frigid the nights are in the barn. It's similar to being in a freezer. You would think the roof should keep the cold out. Instead, the metal seems to attract the icicles. Hang me up on the rafters, and I could be a leg of lamb."

Our big, green edifice is somewhat unusual. Originally, built as an indoor riding arena with stalls on the outside of the two longest ends. It has a veterinary-operating facility at one end, and vet-delivery clinic — where the new foals are born. It is all made of metal with a roof approximately sixty feet tall at the center. The barn is enormous. However, as I say, it is cold, cold, and some more cold.

The riding arena portion is large enough to hold horse shows. I understand they once had major show jumping events held here. Now, trainers Angela and Duke erected temporary stalls, where they keep the moms and babies during the nights. Might be practical, but someone forgot the blankets – or, at least, they forgot mine.

Our barn is by far the largest in Cummings Valley and stands out as a landmark. Some old-timers claim the structure is an eye sore. Again, I'm not sure what the ranchers mean.

"All I can say is that it's damn cold during the winter, and I have no idea, whether it will hell in the summer or not."

Nina says, "Let's walk. We need the exercise. We both must get stronger."

"You are right," I tell Nina. She always talks to me in a way that makes me have pride, and she helps me want to work.

"Tonight, I'll try to get a blanket for you. The others who sleep in the barn have blankets. Why not you?"

"Yea, why not?" I'm trying to appear grown up – however, merely sound stupid. Nina says I act out because I'm figuring out how to fit in.

The real reason, I am forgotten—all the blankets are far too big. At first, they were so large they worried the blanket would smother me. Now, they worry the blankets will put too much weight on me – I will be injured. No one has bothered to cut one down to size.

Both Nina and I have fallen off the radar on the ranch. It is not that her dad, Mr. Torres, is not a good man; he is. Even so, he is under the gun.

"My father got the job because of Angela. He came from Mexico, without any experience and given this opportunity. He has learned as he went along. Nonetheless, he is threatened. He knows he has to produce major winners off this farm, otherwise the Dovatos will blame him." Nina tells me.

Nina and I only get about an hour a day together during the week. On weekends, we might sneak two or three hours. I believe we are soul mates. We look out for each other.

Nina's mother abandoned her, and ran off with another man shortly after Nina's birth. He was the previous farm manager, making matters worse. Now, her mom never comes around — unless she reaches her hand out for money. Takes the little income Marty of the two children exist on day-to-day.

Nina told me, "My mom didn't want to be around me, because I'm a cripple. I am not one of the pretty people. And my mother says dad is a loser; he's only going to work for a living."

"I tell her – Nina, you are beautiful; your mom's a loser. Anyone who doesn't want to be around you is undeserving, nor entitled to her beauty."

While Nina and I play together, Mr. Torres and Tommy work with the foals in my yard. Nina and I stand together—separated from all the others.

No one comes over to teach us. No one plays with us either.

# Chapter 3

**New Year's**.  Nina eighth birthday fell on January 8th.  My birthday came a few days before hers without fanfare.  Tommy was given a big birthday celebration on his day, but Nina's dad was called away to a meeting in Paso Robles on hers.

He got back late.  Marty give to understand that this year's crop of two-year-olds had to perform or Catrina and Tyler Dovato are going to close this farm.  Kentucky and Paso Robles are performing with many stake winners.  Our Tehachapi breeding facility is not.

This ranch is not paying for itself, and Tyler will not tolerate losses.

"I didn't even get a cake or any present.  I know my dad's on the hot seat; it still hurts," Nina cried to me.

"What will happen to you if they sell the farm?"

"I don't know.  Could be that we'll go back to Mexico?"

Nina's mother raced in and out for about ten minutes, just long enough to tell Marty he was really a loser and to snub Nina.  No gift — none at all. What a mother.

Her dad finally offered to get her a dog for a belated birthday gift, but Nina declined saying, "I'm her friend.  I want to spend my time with him, not with some dumb dog."

During a visit at the farm on a chilly February afternoon, her aunt Angela brought a beautiful dress as a gift. Nonetheless, Nina left it on her bed in favor of her tattered jeans and a sweatshirt, so she could spend time with me.

"Aunt Angela, come visit my best friend."

Angela always made time for her niece when she came to the ranch. Angela and Nina walked slowly hand-in-hand out to where we, as friends, unfailingly meet. Angela stood cordial and polite. However, it was easy to see the disappointment in her eyes.

"Two broken forms," Angela thought.

Nina and I spent the afternoon frolicking as we did most days, playing together.

I am, by all accounts, still pitifully small for my age, and segregated from the others. Disappointment, when it came to me, was always widespread.

When I was not with Nina, I soured alone. Painfully alone. However, rather than mope, I spent my time exercising. Nina appreciated work — so I walked and jogged.

"I may be the smallest and the slowest, but I don't give a damn. I'm going to offer everything I can to grow to my body and mind."

The Dovatos were becoming historical among American breeding operations. Four of the top contenders for the Kentucky Derby were bred at a Dovato Farm. Unfortunately, one came from the Kentucky nursery and three from Paso Robles. None, here at Tehachapi.

Stabled in Paso was the nation's leading sire No Rainbows, who sired seventeen stake's winners last year. He has two horses favored in the Derby in May. Furthermore, Dovato Farms houses Avenger, a champion grass stallion that is producing outstanding foals, including five stake's horses last year and another contender for the Derby.

Finally, Dovato's Bart is dropping California's the best sprinters. The Bart is also being bred to quarter horses – making additional income for the Dovato Breeding Farms. He is having success, throwing winners in both categories.

The final showcase at Dovato Farms in Paso Robles is Triple Crown winner No Rain, who won more money than any other horse of all times.

He won 67 times without a loss. He retired sound. Nina's father says he could have raced longer; however, the Dovatos wanted to breed him.

"Unfortunately, No Rain has failed to produce any major winners in his first two crops, and all of his horses have been small," Nina told me.

She might be only eight-years-old; however, Nina is the daughter of a farm manager, who lives breeding.  Nina might be crooked-legged; nonetheless, she is bright as a tack.

"Three strikes and you're out," Nina explains to me. "Last year's foals by No Rain were way too small."

She hunched her shoulders. "They have given up on him, just as they're going to give up on daddy."

"Are you sure?" I asked.

"They are only breeding No Rain to ten mares this year.  Each mare bred stands at least seventeen hands.  They are trying to see whether giant mares will help.  Five of the mares are by No Rainbows.  Daddy says they've really given up."

"No, I mean, have they given up on your daddy?"

"Dad says they are buying more land in Paso Robles, and are going to jettison this farm and him.  I don't know where we'll go next year."

Marty Torres walked silently up beside his daughter without her hearing him.

"Nina, sweetie," said her dad, "Don't worry about things like that. We do not know that for sure.  I haven't given up."

Her dad is a good man, who works from four a.m. until eight p.m. every day. Seven days a week. He has little time to spend with Nina. However, he always made sure she has breakfast, lunch and dinner, and clean clothes. He loves her and his son. He just did not have time.

Time and love are what Nina needed most.

"To be with him, Tommy and I have learned we need to spend our afternoon and early evenings with the horses. We've made them our lives. Tommy runs after him. Every day. I just can't keep up."

Nina Torres learned to ride almost as early as she had learned to walk. She has a big, pony-horse named Tough Stuff. He had been retired from the racetrack after an injury.

"Tough Stuff used to be the pony horse for trainer Duke Snyder, who trains all of Dovato Farms great stake's winners," Nina told me. After he was retired, Duke gave Tough Stuff to Nina, because the gelding was such a "sweetheart."

Early on, Nina looked smaller than a midget riding the gelding; nevertheless, he taught her.

These days Nina rides her trusty mount as I jog alongside her. She never grumbles I'm "going too slowly."

"Don't go too far with him," Marty Torres tells his daughter every afternoon. Away, we would go. Nina knows all the routes through Cummings Valley, and we jog miles. For Nina, I would go, go, and go some more.

The Valley is indeed beautiful. It sits in a basin surrounded by mountains. "There are more criminals per capita in Cummings Valley than any place in the world," her dad jokes. That is simply because the third oldest prison in California, Tehachapi Men's Prison, stands at one end. At another end is Stallion Springs, a resort. We are sort of in the middle.

Nina introduced me to everything. We are inseparable. We might be slow; we might gimp along, but we have each other.

There were many days in the summer that we don't get back until well after dark. Everyone on the Mesa recognizes Nina Torres. Everyone watches out for her. Because of Nina, everyone knew me. Like I say, we are inseparable.

"It's already August and I go back to school next week," she told me. I thought we both were going to cry. The summer is already over. We both spent the warm months together — growing up.

School came, and so did loneliness for me. Yes, I see Nina every afternoon, but it is not enough. We do not have time for our daylong jaunts.

"Come on," she would tell me, "We have time to jog an hour double-time." So, I learned to pick up the pace. It hurts a bit, but for Nina, I will do whatever – only to be around her.

Then, came December – again. There was no early Christmas present. Word came down from on high the property would be sold.

All the horses divided into two categories. If you were good enough you went to Paso Robles. If you were not – hit the bricks.

"Dad says we're going to stay here until the farm is sold. Duke has offered dad a job at the track," Nina explained.

The only good thing about December is I am allowed to stay on with my Nina. I learned, not much later, that meant I needed to find a new home, as well. Alternatively, be turned into glue – whatever that means. I am a loser, they tell me – one way or another.

Too small, too slow.

# Chapter 4

**Unknown Certainty.** Was it the end of the fairytale or the beginning of another?

Perhaps, I should start our story over. Maybe, I forgot to tell one important fact. Or, perhaps, more than one – for that matter.

First, I forgot to tell you my name. I am called **Tehachapi**. That is right; my name is Tehachapi. I am dubbed after the small town in the mountains where I live. About two hours from Los Angeles. No beaches near here; however, plenty of dear and wild life.

Nina named me. She loved me from the start.

Second, although I consider myself a brother to Nina; nevertheless, I am a two-year-old colt by Kentucky Derby winner No Rain, out of the mare Ms. Mary.

I just had my two-year-old birthday on January 1st. All of us horses are a year older that day; whether we are born five minutes after the New Year's, or whether our birthday is in June.

I was born the first Saturday in May, on Kentucky Derby day. Two years ago. I chose the worst time of all to be born. So the story goes, whether it is true or not, I do not remember –I first stumbled to my feet as the gun went off signaling the start of the Derby. Nina did not witness horse racing's biggest event that year; she was in the stall waiting for my birth when my mother Ms. Mary delivered.

Nina says the lads that helped in the birthing lamented, "This guy isn't even worth missing the last race at the Pomona Fair, and, certainly, not missing the Kentucky Derby."

No Rainbows' son won a hard battle down the stretch that day to pull out a head victory in the Derby. The colt later finished second in the Preakness and third in the Belmont.

I've told you quite a bit about my dad, No Rain, who himself stood only fifteen hands. That is very small for a horse racing. The mighty No Rain used to look like a no-account himself in the stall.

There were stories about fans at the track making fun of him. My dad would turn himself into a monster in the stretch – 67 times he won against the odds. He raced against No Rainbows time after time, and each time trounced him.

My father raced five more years after No Rainbows had gone to stud. He raced every three weeks, and sometimes more often. He retired without a pimple on him. Those around my father said he could have won races for another year or so; but the Dovatos were anxious to have babies by him.

"My mom wasn't quite as magnanimous. Yes, mom is good size and had ability; she was considered, generally, lazy."

"She ended up winning four races. Mom too was a loser until the beautiful Angela Torres (Nina's aunt) got on her for Angela's first ride at Hollywood Park. Until Angela, she was even a decent horse racing. Mom, similar to Duke Snyder, fell in love with Angela. Because of mother's love of Angela, she tried. She won three lower rank claiming races."

"So, I guess many would have predicted I wouldn't amount to much. Angela was hoping that my dad's 'will to win' would perk up my racing ability. Unfortunately, my dad's size got in the way."

A couple of days ago, Nina pulled out the tape measure to see how tall I am. She found out I was not quite 14 hands.

"He's too small to be a horse racing," Marty told his daughter.

Nina is now nine years old, but has the maturity and understanding of someone much older and wiser. She spent her formative years at the school of hard knocks – a breeding farm.

"Where is it written, dad?" She questioned.

"Where is what written?"

"Where does it say that you have to be a certain height to be a race horse? No Rain was superior to No Rainbows. Who is tallest?"

"Tehachapi is a pony – not a horse," her dad recoiled.

Nina knew full-well No Rainbows is a majestic colt that stands 17 hands, more than nine inches taller than No Rain. No Rainbows is the grandest of them all. He is statuesque.

If someone asked how you should paint a picture of the greatest horse racing, they pictured him.

No Rainbows' perfect physique, proportions and confirmation makes him the sire of sires. Indeed, No Rain fails in comparison. Only, on the track was No Rain bigger than life.

"You know what I mean. I understand you love Tehachapi. Even so, he's always been such a little tyke. He had troubles at birth. He has never out-raced one of the farm's crippled mares."

"Dad, what are they going to do with him?"

"I don't know."

"See how much they want for him?"

"Honey, I don't have any extra money. I might have to go to the track and start over again. We will have trouble getting by on what I earn at the barn. There just is no extra money."

"Find out how much they want for him. Will you?"

Marty, knowing he could not win, nodded yes.

# Chapter 5

**A Name Change.** Only a few days later, events gave Nina and me a break. It was one of those arctic, blustery, January days where the wind howled through the pines. An unmemorable day to most. Nonetheless, scourge of a day was the second that I will never forget.

I must remember how things came down, so I could report them to Nina, who was off at school. An eternity later, when she came home and finally came out to play, I told her.

"Duke and Angela Snyder, the Dovatos and your father had a big meeting. As you know, I can have freedom here at the ranch, so I meandered along behind them.

"Out of the paddock again, huh?"

"Tyler reported he is acquiring a billion-dollar aerospace company, and wants to create as much cash as possible for the purchase. He wants to sell our ranch immediately.

"He offered our ranch to Duke for three million dollars cash. Sounds like a lot of carrots. Nevertheless, that would include the ranch, one hundred and sixty acres, the houses and horses. All twelve horses, left on the farm — including me — would stay with Duke.

"He was also offered ownership of No Rain and ten mares in foal to the little stallion. They are presently at the Paso Robles farm. Duke says he still has faith that No Rain can make a decent stallion."

Nina already heard everything I reported to her from her aunt. Additionally, she told me that Duke had wangled three more No Rain two-year-olds, and seven No Rain yearlings.

"I guess the price went up a bit for everything that was included," Nina reported. Duke has been immensely successful as a trainer, and has stockpiled a ton of cash – plus he's getting additional financing from his good friend, Tony, who is Catrina Dovato's father.

"Hooray," I scream. I get to stay with my Nina.

"What's more, my dad is going to be instructed as a horse trainer. He will manage the farm for Duke."

Duke Snyder and Angela have become immensely popular and successful in the years since No Rain won the Kentucky Derby and the Triple Crown. Duke now has horses in training at Hollywood Park and Santa Anita; Churchill downs in Kentucky, in New York and Florida. He won more stakes races last year than any other trainer in America.

He also works part-time as a private investigator for Cory Bentley, a famed criminal lawyer. To say the least, Duke Snyder has his hands full. Duke is a private pilot, who flies a twin Cessna jet, making his travels easier.

"He and Angela are going to live here part-time, because Duke's duties now take him throughout the country, working with his animals and for stake races. Angela is so good with young horses. She is going to be responsible for the breaking and training of the two-year-olds," Nina told me.

"Does that mean that Angela will ride me?"

"Yes, I suppose."

"Why not you?"

"I guess they figure I would get hurt," she said despondently.

"No way, I won't hurt you."

"You don't have any idea what it's like having someone on your back. The horses always buck hard. Experienced riders need to start out the new colts."

"Not me. I won't buck you off if you are the rider. If someone else tries to get on me, I'll send them flying."

"Not Angela. She's wonderful. You will love her. I am going to be jealous when she gets to ride you. Don't you dare hurt her," Nina said.

"Okay."

Tough Stuff, Nina and I got to go for a two-hour jog through Cummings Valley. Gallivanting is our favorite thing to do.

**The next morning.** Duke and Angela stayed on overnight in the big house on our ranch. Nina told me the home had four bedrooms upstairs, including an immense master. Downstairs, there was a gigantic living room, which overlooked by the open walkway leading to the bedrooms above. The elegant farm home had a den, picturesque dining room with a bay window overlooking the ranch, and wonderful kitchen. Nina was obviously in love with the abode, because Tommy, her father and her lived in a much smaller manager's house on the farm.

On a walk, trainer Duke Snyder saw me. "This one is by No Rain," said Duke to Angela.

"He's actually fairly big for a yearling."

Angela told him, "No, he's a two-year-old. He's nearly 14 hands tall. Everyone has already given up on him, except Nina."

"He's one of the horses we purchased?"

"Well, I guess technically he is. By definition, he is one of the horses left on the farm. However, Nina and Tehachapi have been inseparable since he was born on Kentucky Derby day. She spends every waking hour with him. They jog through Cummings Valley – as if they own it. "

"Well I presume he's going to be a little small, even by No Rains standards. A midget to race."

Duke bent over and picked up my feet, one at a time. He inspected me as no one other than Nina had done in more than a year. He was gentle and kind.

He touched my knees by running his hands over them as he bent the tiny legs. He had Angela walk me away from him about fifteen feet. She turned around and walk me directly back toward him.

"He may be small, but very similar to his dad. He walks perfectly. Furthermore, he has the right feet, good cannons, and even though a dwarf, his proportions are perfect."

"Perfect," I thought. No one had ever said anything about me was perfect.

"You'll get an argument from Nina if you tell her that he's too tiny to do anything," Angela said truthfully.

"While the two-year-olds have grown-up frolicking in large paddocks, this guy has put on the miles, jogging aside your old pony horse Tough Stuff. Nina talks to Tehachapi as you and I converse with each other."

"Are you going to break him?"

"Yes, certainly. I will involve Nina in the process, so she can learn. My guess, Tehachapi will allow her on his back without a squawk."

Of course, Angela was correct. I thought, "Maybe Nina is right that she talks to horses as well. Moreover, Nina says Duke is a horse whisperer, whatever that is."

Sometimes I hear Nina's whisper, but most time we just talk to each other.

At least, now, I have an understanding of what to expect.

Nothing was said about riding me that day or the next. However, three days later when Nina came out of the barn to get me in the afternoon, she wore strange pants, which I had seen on some other riders before. They were not jeans. They were close fitting, with a solid fabric on the butt.

"What are you wearing? You look strange?"

"Oh this is my new jockey outfit. Now that I'm going to be a horse jockey, I needed to have the right clothing. Angela got them for me. Aren't they cool?"

"Cool no. But you are."

"You're strange."

I let that pass.

I asked her, "Does this mean you get to ride me?"

"Tehachapi, sometimes you are dense. Of course, I am your jockey in training."

"Am I a horse racing in training?"

"No one thinks so, other than us. But, yes."

I could have died from excitement. It was one of the only times in my life, so far, that anyone considered me anything other than a loser. No one knew it yet, but I was going to try harder than any of these suckers—an attempt to be a successful horse racing.

The racing community has now given up on my father, No Rain, because he is too small. He is not large enough to have sons that can race successfully.

"At least that's what people think."

# Chapter 6

**Smart as a Whip**. Angela and Nina did not waste any time. Nina was given the chore of leading me through an obstacle course. Angela had set up cones on the ground, and the horses led slowly through the meandering route.

"You and Tehachapi do that well, better than any of the two-year-olds," Angela said.

"Tehachapi and I have been doing simple stuff for two years. Would you like to see him go through it, forwards and backwards, without a lead rope?"

"Yes," said Angela in shock.

"Honey..." said Marty. "Don't expect too much of your little guy."

Nina shrugged her shoulders in despair at her father's cutting remark. Nina made a zig-zag sign to me, which I instantly understood.

I kicked up my heels, and paraded forwards and retraced the steps through the cones.

"Unbelievable," cried Angela. "Wait until Duke sees that."

Marty looked on, gaining new respect for his daughter.

"I certainly didn't teach Tehachapi that move. Honestly, I have not touched him in well over a year. Tehachapi has been left totally to Nina."

"And I suspect Nina has been left totally to Tehachapi, because of your overall devotion to the farm," Angela said.

Her brother shrugged his shoulders, nodding yes. "I understand what Tommy needs. A little girl... I love; don't know the first thing to do to help her."

Angela understood. Her expression sober with concern.

While the other horses continued their lead rope training, Nina, her dad and I went into the barn's arena. Marty Torres brought out a small horse racing saddle.

"It's much smaller than the Western saddle I use on Tough Stuff. All we use on race horses," Nina told me. "No horn for me to hold on to, if you goof around."

I already had a good understanding, because I had seen riders on some of the two-year-olds from the previous crop the year before.

Marty Torres put the saddle on my back and touched me on the hip telling me to stand still.

I stood.

Marty tugged a leather device around my girth and tightened it. At first, it felt as if he was sucking all the air out of me.

I jumped.

"I told you to stand still."

"Dad, easy. He will follow instructions as long as he understands what you are doing. Just go slow with him." Nina said giving her elder instructions.

It was the child teaching the adult.

Marty listened.

"Okay boy, I'm sorry Tehachapi. I'll slow it down. Let's all learn together." Marty Torres was a tender man, who had fallen out of training as a father. Angela had put Marty and Nina together, so dad and daughter could reconnect. She thought the most important thing was their relationship – getting fixed. Certainly more vital than whatever happened to Tehachapi.

Angela also concluded long before the exercise started that afternoon that Tehachapi would be Nina's training device. The colt was so small he would not make a horse racing, but Nina could learn with him.

Once saddled, Nina told me to follow her back to the arena where Angela still was leading the dunces through the cones. I walked directly behind her – two steps behind as I had been taught. Nina had taught me to walk far enough behind, so I could stop without running her over. She limped and often took a bad step.

"Angela, here we are."

"Take him through the cones with his saddles on."

Nina instructed, "Tehachapi, gallop."

I did as told. This time I galloped over the course, and retraced my steps to where my brown-eyed girl stood. I did not touch one of the cones.

"Easy." I said. At this, I am best.

"Because I'm small, I'm also extremely maneuverable," I told her. She informed me with her eyes she understood.

Angela and Marty both had their jaws wide open. They looked as if they were trying to catch flies. I guess the two adults were amazed, I could so easily turn right and left, and do it at a gallop.

Nina told Angela, "Tehachapi is ready to be ridden. You are going to have to teach me what is expected of him under saddle. If I understand, I'll do it."

Angela rode at an early age. She had been raised on horseback by her father, and had done dressage, and later show jumping. Angela herself had always ridden large horses. She understood. She truly understood Nina.

"Let's have him walk all the way around the arena going left."

I caught the instructions and actually started out before Nina. Two strides later, she quickly caught up and walked beside me.

"I don't know what's coming next, exactly? Tehachapi, listen carefully."

The other two-year-olds were tucked into stalls. This is the first time in my two-year-old life that I am going to get to start before the others.

"How much do you think Tehachapi weighs?" Angela asked.

Marty said, "That's a good question. He is very small and on the scrawny side. Maybe, 500 – 600 pounds? I don't know."

Angela queried, "I am concerned about weight on his back. Do you think we would be better to wait until he is three years old to break him? Let him grow up a little more?"

"No!" exclaimed Nina. "You tell me what you want and I'll do it. I only weigh sixty-five pounds. That won't hurt him."

Angela looked at Marty Torres for answers. Both were not certain what to do.

Without words, Nina pulled on the saddle and Tehachapi's mane, pushing him over to a fence, which separated the arena from the remainder of the barn. Nina struggled up the fence with her brace.

Marty and Angela were talking quietly about the situation, and paying no notice to Tehachapi. Nina was blocked from view of the adults, because I was standing between them.

"Easy friend," said Nina, tickling me about my mane as she had done for two years. "I'm getting up, be careful with me."

Then, Nina was aboard. She felt as light as a bug. I didn't know what to expect. I thought it might hurt me. She was a feather. It was good to have her on my back. I could imagine running Cummings Valley with her aboard.

Nina was smart. She was holding my mane. Not pulling on my mouth with the rein-device. It felt very strange. Her fingers on my mane felt good.

Suddenly, Angela and Marty looked at Tehachapi and Nina, who were circling them.

"Oh, My God," said Angela.

"No big deal," said Nina. "He's a dream. I just need some help teaching him what to do with the reins. We have not worked with that yet. Obviously, I understand from riding Tough Stuff and other ponies. This nerd has no idea."

I said, "Watch it, or I'll send you flying."

Nina smiled.

"What can you do with him?"

"What would you like?"

"Can you jog him around the arena, holding on to his mane?"

"Sure. Tehachapi, gallop."

Off we went.

# Chapter 7

**Following the Instructions?**  The next 60 days went quickly. I found the time exciting.  I was not alone.  During the daytime, while Nina was at school, Angela made hours to work with me.

Working with both Angela and Nina became exhilarating.

Many of the two-year-olds became exhausted by the work—not accustomed to following a trainer's routine.  They wanted to jump and play in their large paddocks.  Uncomfortable being forced to gallop with a jockey on their back.

Most of the two-year-olds could not stand being left in a stall most of the day. They had grown up in large paddocks outside.

My life was a bed of roses.  I got out of my stall once in the morning.   And I was fed better than ever before, including oats routinely.  In the afternoon, I would get out to work with Nina.

We would spend our off -time running through Cummings Valley.  My legs no longer felt creaky as they had in early childhood. I believe the long gallops Nina and I took helped strengthen the tinny limbs.

Once her dad, Marty Torres, had built a half-mile track around our farm Nina and I broke it in by playing "race horse." Nina pretended she was a jockey on Tough Stuff, and I would race along besides her trying to nip her mount at the wire. We must have played the game a hundred times.

"Angela and Duke say we can't go too fast; even so, we can gallop miles," Nina said.

Then, Nina started bringing a stopwatch, and we would time ourselves. We were not allowed to go fast; nevertheless, Nina reasoned we could keep track of how fast we tracked.

"We beat yesterday's time," she would report.

"Now that your dad is putting more sand down on the track my feet feel better. Makes it much easier to pick up the time," I told her.

Marty Torres had brought in a mixture of materials that Duke had procured at great expense and after considerable thought. Cummings Valley received snow, torrential rains and wintry storms. At times of the year the track would be arid and another portion of the year it would be a gigantic mud puddle.

Nina's dad was a patient man, who had learned you do things right the first time. He spent time each day considering where water would accumulate during heavy rains. Marty built two small lakes to catch runoff.

He also installed sprinklers around the track, so he could water expertly and easily. He procured a tractor and drag. Now, we were pretty much a genuine racetrack.

At night, Marty, Angela, Tommy, and Nina checked every hoof, every tendon, and went over all the two-year-olds with a fine-tooth comb. Even the smallest problem was reported, so Marty could make adjustments to the track's surface.

The biggest man I have ever seen, named Scrap, was brought to the ranch for a one-week grooming course. He weighed over 400 pounds – he is nearly as big as I am.

"Yes, I weigh more than he does, maybe," I told Nina.

"I don't think so," she said. "You better eat more – and he better eat less."

Scrap was now an assistant trainer at Hollywood Park, under Duke. Scrap for years was the groom of the best horse racings in Duke Snyder's barn. He groomed the mighty No Rain, No Rainbows, Avenger, and Dovato's Bart.

Scrap was so large he sat directly under a horse while he groomed. He would move from leg to leg.

"He doesn't have to get up, that way," Nina explained to me.

I was the first horse Scrap attended to at our farm. Again, since Scrap was so famous, I enjoyed the honor. Finally, I found myself in the limelight, and I was starting to feel better about life. Scrap was so valuable to the racing stable at Hollywood Park he could not be spared for long from his duties, but Duke believed training Marty Torres and the Cummings Valley staff was invaluable.

"Nina, he is gigantic. However, when he puts that mud-stuff on my legs, what a difference. He also makes my hoofs terrific."

"Yes, Scrap is about the only person who Duke doesn't question. If Scrap says a horse is sound, then it is sound.

Later, that day, Scrap pointed at me, Tehachapi – "The little runt has the soundest legs of all the two-year-olds."

Angela told Scrap, "Nina doesn't know when to back off of him. She just goes and goes. Tehachapi tracks wherever she points – for miles."

Angela went on, "When I check Tehachapi in the morning, I'm sure he's going to be lame. Nevertheless, his legs are ice cubes."

Marty responded, "Those two have tracked 1,000 miles up here since he was a yearling. They click off five here as other horses work a quarter."

"I don't know, but he certainly is sound. Part of his soundness is how little he weighs. He probably doesn't weigh a ham sandwich," said Scrap.

**The First Works.** Duke was home and told Angela they would work nine of the two-year-olds that morning, and nine more the next day.

"I want to get a handle on several things. First, I want to see how the track works. Second, want to understand how far along these are in comparison to the two-year-olds coming into the track."

Angela said, "Marty's done a great job on the track at the farm. I feel better about working young horses than at Hollywood. How fast are you going with them?"

"You know them best – what you think? Duke questioned.

"I would say most of them should check in about 50 seconds. There are two nice ones, which shipped in from a Kentucky-owner's farm that may go faster."

"How about the runt? Nina is bugging me to breeze him." Duke said, looking cross-eyed.

"You better not let Nina hear you say he's a runt, or she will be in your ear."

"Is he as much of a dud as he looks?"

"Ask Scrap about Tehachapi's soundness? Going a half mile, he will be very slow. Going a mile he'll be right there with them," Angela proclaimed.

Nina came over and talked to me. "Tehachapi just do your best – don't worry what Duke says. It will be okay."

I was selected to go last of the nine in the group for tomorrow. That sentence equated to being diagnosed as a worst horse on the farm. Luckily, for me, Nina chose to breeze me. A first, for both of us.

"We'll surprise some of the folks when the works start getting longer," Nina told me. She said she needed to get her right leg strengthened so she could breeze me more than a mile.

The first day's works were "not fantastic," reported Nina. One colt, from a Kentucky farm, went in 47 seconds for the half-mile. All the rest were around 50 seconds — some slower.

When I awoke this morning, I found the day to be icy. The first works slated to start at eleven a.m. This would allow Duke the time to watch the video conferencing of works from Hollywood Park, and Santa Anita, as well as Eastern tracks.

"Only one horse went faster than 50 seconds for a half-mile yesterday," Nina repeated to me. "A sprinter named Tim's Bart, who's bred to go fast and early. He went in 47 and 2/5ths easy. Duke is sending him to the track with two others next week."

"How fast do you want us to work?"

"I don't know how fast you can do it."

"I'm not certain either, but I know the further we go the better. I think we should keep going a mile. I can go two miles, but Duke and Angela might get mad at us. A mile, we should do easily."

"Let's play it by ear," Nina said. "I'm not like Angela. I don't have a clock in my head. They're allowing me to wear a watch, but it's difficult to look and ride."

Eight other horses went out that morning and Angela had those clocked around 50 seconds for half-mile. Every one of them was blowing when they came back to the barn.

Duke sat in a viewing box above the track, where he could view all the horses' works. Angela came and sat next to Duke when tiny Nina, brace and all, brought Tehachapi onto the track for his work.

Nina was not intimidated. She backtracked me, in the opposite direction to normal track traffic for a quarter-mile.

"Let's get you good and warm before we start working," she said.

"Chilly today. You are right. We needed to warm up," I told her.

"When the horn goes off, we're going to start. We are going to pick up at a good pace – without a rush. Once we get in our groove, we will keep working. When we hit the half-mile point, we will decide whether we need to stop or go on."

"I think we both have enough stamina, even working, to go a mile," I told her.

"We'll see. I hope you are right. I've seen all the rest blowing hard when they came back from a half-mile. And I don't know about my leg."

"Oh, yea. I forgot. To me, you're perfect," I told her. I meant it.

Nina turned me and headed back to the starting point. As she approached the starting point, she heard the horn and took off from the poll.

We did a quarter with ease. Felt amazing to both of us.

"You are working beautifully Tehachapi. As never before. You are great. You're really striding out," she told me.

As we moved past Duke and Angela, both studied us. Duke was focused more on me—Angela totally on her niece.

"Nina has a perfect form. In 60 days, she's learned how to ride horse racings. Look at how adroitly she handles Tehachapi, and the signals she's sending him through her hands, Angela said.

Duke did not hear her.

"Look at him. At that little bugger – Tehachapi. He floats above the ground like his daddy. His ears are attentively listening to his rider. He's actually floating."

No Rain had always been such a marvel, because it appeared, he never touched the ground. He seemed to have all four feet off the ground at all time. Even though, No Rain was small at barely 15 hands, he covered a lot of ground because of his floating stride.

"I haven't seen another No Rain colt with the same action," said Duke.

Duke and Angela both had stopwatches fixed on the tiny colt. As he finished the half-mile, Duke clocked him in 47 and 4/5ths, which was the second fastest time for the two days.

"What's she doing?" questioned Duke, as Nina continued with Tehachapi.

"She's obviously working further," said Angela.

"Will have to talk to her about following instructions," said the trainer.

Tehachapi, unabated, continued on his march around the oval. Clear to the trained eye he was not struggling, but enjoying every second of the work.

Horse and gal floated above the ground like angels anointing Cummings Valley. Tehachapi worked a mile that morning, and would have worked another – except, little Nina eased him up at the end of his journey.

"I don't believe it. They just worked in 1:35 and 3/5ths. Their second-half was quicker than their first," said Duke. "I'm going to strangle her."

Angela, standing, said, "The hell you are. You are going to complement Tehachapi, and then very quietly explained to Nina why she shouldn't have done what she did. She's nine years old, and is merely trying to make her horse appear to be the best."

"I realize with you aboard the other horses are carrying 109. What does she weigh? That's quite a weight break for Tehachapi."

"I think she weighs 65 pounds."

"Well, a 44-pound weight break is significant, but still. Let's go find out if his legs are going to fall off."

Nina did what she was trained to do. We slowed to a gallop and into a walk. She took us all the way around the course, another half-mile, cooling me out.

By the time I made the trip back to the barn, Duke and Angela were waiting. Marty—with his hands in his pockets—joined Nina's brother Tommy.

"Dad what did she do wrong?" asked Tommy.

"She didn't listen. She was told to work a half-mile, and she worked Tehachapi twice as far. That's unacceptable," Marty responded.

"Get off him," said Duke angrily.

Angela put her hand tenderly on Duke's shoulder and said, "She's nine."

"If she wants to make it until she is ten-years-old, she'd better learn to listen – and now!"

Nina understood what she had done wrong. Like most felons, she knew it before she did it. Even so, she was tired of having people put Tehachapi down. Also, in her heart-of-hearts, she was certain she hadn't hurt him.

The little girl with the big brown eyes slid down off Tehachapi and landed on her good leg.

"What do you think you did wrong?" asked Duke.

"The last half-mile I worked was a little too quick," she said — thinking fast.

"Say what?"

"My last half-mile was a little quick."

"How far were you to work?"

"A half-mile. However, I wanted to be sure he was warm before I worked him fast," said Nina with a straight face.

"Now, I've heard it all," said Duke. "The first half-mile you were just warming up?"

"Yes."

"If you ran a race at Hollywood Park as fast as you worked a mile, you could win some of the maiden races there. You worked too far, way too quick. This is his first work. If he has any legs tomorrow it will be a wonder," Duke criticized.

"I'm sorry. He will be fine. We really did not go fast for him. He's used to galloping three and four miles," said the nine-year-old with all sincerity. "Half-mile is excessively short for him to show anything. Even a mile isn't a test."

"Do you understand Angela is a trainer here, along with your dad, who is learning?"

"Yes."

"Good.  You are in training, as well.  You are in training to be a rider.  When you are given a time for a distance, your job is to bring your horse in right on that time.  You understand?"

"Yes – I've got it.  No one gave me a time.  You guys just gave me a stopwatch."

Duke thought this nine-year-old was exactly like his aunt.

In ten minutes after I had my bath, Nina and I were playing.  My legs were fine, and I felt that I had not done enough.

"I think we got their attention.  Now they know; you are not such a dud," said Nina winking at me.

It was Duke, who was on all fours, smeared the mud on me that afternoon.  He had cornered Nina, and was ready to point out how wrong she was.  However, my legs were ice cold.

Duke checked my knees and my tendons as he had done before.  Absolutely – nothing wrong.

"Tehachapi is so easy on himself because of the way he goes," said Nina.  "Many of the others make the ground shake when they go.  He barely leaves footprints.  Someday, measure his strides from where he takes off to where he lands, and you will see the amount of ground he covers."

Duke took out a tape measure that afternoon.  It has long been known, when you work a two-year-old, they start growing.  I was now fourteen and a quarter hands.

"Angela, maybe, Tehachapi will finish out at 15 hands like his daddy.  We're going to work him once more, and, next, he will take 60 days off – let him grow up," said Duke.

I considered a layoff a good thing, because I was not ready to go to the track and be away from Nina. I understood she would not go with me – I had some growing to do emotionally before I can accept being distant from her.

Marty asked, "How is it possible a horse we all thought was such a throw out, turned around so quickly. He couldn't beat a snail to the other end of the paddock growing up?"

"We still don't know how useful he will be," said Duke. He had so little weight on him compared to the others; he still may be no good. Nina is correct Tehachapi has a unique way of going that he inherited from his father."

Angela added, "The other thing – he loves Nina. That precious little girl walks with God."

# Chapter 8

**Better and Better.** Two weeks later Angela was on my back as we floated three-quarters of a mile. Certainly, there was a weight difference. However, I grew used to Angela and her embraces during morning gallops. I loved her attention; for her attitude toward me was much changed from the early days.

She had a pleasing touch, and never jerked on the mouth as my young companion occasionally did. For Nina, I would overlook the pain.

"Angela, Angela, can you hear me?" I asked.

Unlike with my Nina, there was no answer – other than her communication through her expert hands on the reins. I learned most humans communicate with horses through touches.

We floated that morning. Don't know how I learned to float, or where it came from. Once I started to gallop, I glide through the air – outstretched – off the ground and push forward. Didn't do it when I raced the thugs in the paddocks when I was very young.

"I wanted to see how far I can stretch in a continuous stride," I said to myself that morning. Clear to me Angela could not hear me, other than through what I did.

When my stride reached too far, and became even longer, Angela would apply the faintest touch, which signaled me to return to reality.

My Nina returned home in the afternoon with a million questions.

"Well tell me, how was it? Did you miss me?"

"Did I? Of course."

"How did it feel with Angela on your back, breezing fast?"

"Well, she gallops me in the morning and gives me instruction. So really, I've learned her weight. I missed you, but it was fine."

"How fast did you go?"

"I don't know. She didn't tell me. I think she was happy. She gave me a pat on my neck when we finished. However, she didn't talk to me, so I don't know."

"I'll ask her. I'll be right back."

Off went Nina, away from my stall. I should have told her, I breezed strong as the wind. She would have stayed, and talked with me. I get too little time with her when she is in school. Her dad gives her chores to do, so now I get to spend even less time with my Nina.

Furthermore, she gets up on some of the other horses now.

"You did 1 minute 13 seconds for three-quarters of a mile. Angela is incredibly pleased. She says you are not going to be a sprinter though. She thinks you may be quite good as a distant horse."

"What's a distance horse?"

"From what I can gather from overhearing her talking to Uncle Duke, it must mean a horse that can run more than a mile."

"Oh Nina, that's what we like to do. We want to run forever. I'm slow, but when I can race into the wind for miles, I have a chance to be good."

Nina explained to me that in America, races are generally no more than a mile and a quarter to a mile and one-half. In Europe, they run further.

"Then Nina, you and I must go to Europe."

She laughed. "I'm only nine. What do you think?"

"I think you can do anything in the world; you want to do. You have taught me that lesson. When I used to stand at the edge of the paddock feeling sorry for myself, you came telling me to pick up my heels. Run further and faster. Keep a running when the others quit."

Nina explained they were going to turn me out in a large paddock in the daytime, so I could run and grow. At night, now that I was a "horse in training." I had a stall – heavy with straw and a warm blanket.

"The nights are not so cold, now that you got me a fancy blanket with my name on it," I told my little Nina. "The others are jealous – they don't get their names on their standard blankets.

"You are going to get a 60-day vacation. I want you to keep galloping, and not merely sleeping in the sun," Nina said instructionally.

"Yes boss," I said winking.

# Chapter 9

**A Scary Place.** As things turned out, the next sixty days were slightly more exciting than merely resting in a large paddock. Indeed, by morning, I would find myself basking in the early sunlight. Soon, Nina would return home. She saddled me with the western type, which was heavier.

Angela mounted Tough Stuff and another pony horse each day to do her farm assignments. Tough Stuff was too old for much for continuous duty. So, Nina she saddled me, and I became her workhorse. Think of it – a horse racing one fine day, and the next Nina's pony horse.

"Be careful with him," Angela warned. "If you want him to be a horse racing, you have to treat him as one."

"Tehachapi and I go for miles. The little things you are giving me to do are nothing compared to what he is accustomed to doing."

In fact, after Nina and I took some of the younger horses on jogs; we had time many days to gallop through Cummings Valley.

"I like being a horse racing. But I love our gallops through Cummings, and have missed them."

We explored different areas than we had before. Both of us wanting to learn more and more.

"This is the way to Bear Valley, Nina told me."

We walked and we walked. We galloped, and we galloped. Day turned to night. We were lost in Bear Valley.

I wondered whether there were really bears here. Someone had given the picturesque place the name.

"Daddy," said Nina over her cell phone to Marty Torres. "Tehachapi and I are lost. We are in Bear Valley. We have taken turns, and jogged across fields. I tried to turn around, but I think we went too far."

It was scary out here. We were in the wilderness. There were creature sounds.

I have never heard before. Sure, the wind howled. That was nothing new. Even so, there were noises, which seemed louder and closer.

Marty Torres asked a few questions and said he would bring his truck with a trailer – "be there soon." Marty knew from what Nina had told him that they had climbed high into the mountains.

"Turn downhill and walk on the side of the street. Stay off the road so a car doesn't hit you guys. Stay downhill, and walk."

"Yes dad," Nina responded.

It seemed like hours, but indeed only a few minutes elapsed before Marty Torres and our Angela picked us up. We met this nice, young lady who had come out of her house when she saw us walking. She had talked to my father on the cell phone and explained right where we were.

"Nina," her dad said when he arrived. It was clear he was angry. However, almost immediately he saw Mary Grice. Mary was beautiful. She stood 5 feet 7 inches, 115 pounds with long blonde hair and blue eyes.

"Daddy always says brown eyes are beautiful. But he sure can't take his eyes off of Mary," said Nina. "He doesn't look so mad anymore."

In fact, Angela had to prod Marty to load Tehachapi in the trailer.

"Marty, it is cold out here.   Let's get loading," Angela encouraged.

The trailer was a new thing to me.  My mother, Ms. Mary, had been brought to the farm before I was born.  I had never seen the inside of a trailer.  It certainly isn't the best time to be learning how to load at nine o'clock at night.

Marty was having some difficulty with me, trying to force me into the trailer.  He was not being unkind, but it was a scary place.

"Let me have the lead rope dad," said Nina.

She took the rope, and hopped up into the black recesses of the two-horse trailer.

"She looks so tiny standing there," said Mary.

I thought, "If my Nina can jump in that damn trailer, what am I making all the fuss about?

"Tehachapi cut the nonsense.  It's only a horse trailer," Nina yelled at me.

"Okay, you are right."

I put one leg up.  Next, I put another leg up.  I was getting in as kids do in a cold swimming pool.

"Come on, it is fine," said Nina with a friendly voice.

After a momentary pause, I made a forward lunge all at once and almost trampled her.  I caught myself in midair.  I was used to being maneuverable, so I sidestepped her.

"Wow.  That was close."

Both of us looked out of the open side window of the horse trailer and saw both Marty and Mary looking intently at each other.

"Marty, get her phone number, and let's get the hell out of here before we all freeze," said Angela chiding her brother.

"Your phone number?"

Mary bounded into action and sprinted into her house. She returned with a card. We found out that Mary bred warmbloods, for the show jumping circuit. Angela wasn't so cold anymore – became interested in the jumpers, because she had catapulted skyward with horses six feet in the air when she did the A-circuit show jumping as a youth.

"Looks as if we both have something to talk about, Mary," said Angela. "Wanted to buy a young warmblood for years and train him to be a jumper. Maybe, my brother and I can come up and visit you in the daytime?"

"Please do," said Mary looking at Marty.

Nina rode with me in the back of the trailer. She was in one stall, and I was in the other. We bumped our way to Cummings Valley farm.

"Dad has been very lonely for long time. Hope Mary is nice. He deserves someone," Nina explained to me.

# Chapter 10

**Love in Cummings Valley.** Mary Grice was not going to let moss grow on the tree. Not too many single women in the Tehachapi Valley. From Mary's point of view, there were no eligible men, who looked as handsome as Marty.

Next afternoon, at about 3:30 p.m., Mary showed up at Cummings Valley farm with an old, dilapidated trailer. When she pulled in by the training barn, we all saw her coming.

Wasn't quite certain who was the most excited Angela or Marty. In addition, clear that Mary was trailing a warmblood in the oversized trailer.

"What do you have there?" inquired Angela.

"This is my most prized three-year-old. Kept him for someone special. I looked you up last night on the Internet, and realized you were doing the professional show jumping circuit before you had to give it up. After, you became a horse racing rider and trainer. Obvious you have talent."

Angela blushed.

"Don't tell her that. It'll go to her head," said Marty. "In all honesty, Angela is special. The best."

Mary swung open the trailer's back door. Marty fastened a lead rope to the tall, Chestnut warmblood. He slowly backed the colt out.

"He's by my champion warmblood stallion, out of my best mare, which is a champion at the Oaks, and won a number of shows in Burbank. This is her first foal. A first for him, as well."

Marty walked him away from the trailer and down the road about forty feet, and turned toward Angela.

"He's not broken yet. Even so, you should see him jump over a fence."

Our fences at Cummings Valley farm were a little more than five feet—had wire-mesh below, so no horse could get out. Certainly, no horse on the farm ever thought of jumping clear of the paddock.

Mary went to the trailer and picked up a long lunge line. She met Marty as he guided the three-year-old colt to Angela. Mary clipped the line on.

"Marty hold him a stride and a half away from the fence," she instructed. Mary turned and went through the gate into the paddock where I was located. I came over inquisitively to find out what was going on.

Mary started to shoo me away, when Nina saw what she wanted.

"Tehachapi give her some room."

I backed up and over toward the side. I still wanted to be near the action, but not too close. Mary was now inside my paddock in a straight line to where her prized animal stood. A fence stood between the horse and Mary.

"Okay Marty, let loose of him."

"Really."

"You bet."

Mary clucked at the three-year-old. With one-step and a graceful arch, he soared over the fence with two feet to spare.

"That's amazing," said Angela.

"I had him over a 6.5-foot fence, and a doubler of over 6 feet each. He jumps effortlessly."

Marty said, "Let me show you around our farm. You can leave him there in the paddock with Tehachapi, unless he will jump out."

"No. My paddocks at home have shorter fences. None of my warmbloods ever jumped out. They could with ease. Just not in their makeup, unless I'm working with them."

I was a midget next to the 18-hand warmblood. He was a good fifteen inches taller than I was. However, unlike the rambunctious two-year-olds, my companion seemed to have a good sense. What's more, he wanted companionship.

At first, I had trouble picking up his speech. Clear he had originated from a different country, with a different language. Shortly, however, we were old pals talking to each other.

"What's that jumping stuff?" I inquired.

"That's what we do. Jump. We take our rider through a course with jumps. The horse that can go the round clear with no rails down is the victor," he explained.

"Oh, that sounds interesting."

"I heard them call you Tehachapi."

"Yep. That's me."

"What do you do?"

"Well, I'm the greatest miler horse racing that you've ever seen. I run and run and run until no one can run anymore."

"That sounds exhausting. I think I will stick with jumping."

I did not get to see my Nina that afternoon. Enjoyed the visit with my paddock guest, but I would much rather be galloping through Cummings Valley with Nina.

"Mary stayed for dinner," said Nina when she came to put me in my stall. "I guess we're going to keep the big guy for a while; he'll hang out with you. Angela is very busy, but she wants to set up a course and see him jump. Mary has agreed to come over – set the course and help Angela in the late afternoons for the next few days."

"Does that mean I don't get to spend time with you?"

"No, we'll hang out. Maybe we can watch him jump a little. Later, we'll go for a gallop."

"Sounds great."

"I think Angela is helping my dad get to know Mary. Angela says daddy is shy. She thinks he is similar to Duke. She says she must get my father get off the dime. Whatever that means."

"Well, Mary isn't shy. She is very friendly and nice. Do you think Angela will buy that warmblood?"

"I don't know. I know Duke has told her to go ahead if she wants it. I guess it's something she has wanted to do for a long time. It reminds her of times past spent with her father."

I was tucked away in my stall; given a kiss on my nose by my Nina. All was right with the world.

# Chapter 11

**A Fanciful Work.** We saw a lot of Mary over the next weeks. In fact, Mary invited Nina and me to spend the night. We galloped over to Bear Valley. This time it was not so mystifying.

It was clear that Mary went out of her way to spend time with Nina. She told her, "Sweetie, I can't have children. Your daddy is so lucky. I had a horse accident when I was younger."

Mary and Nina seemed to have a lot in common. They had both had been lonely at times. At first, I was jealous. I thought it was probably a good thing, because while I was off at the track being a horse racing, Nina would have someone.

Marty and Mary became very tight.

"Lovey-dovey," says Nina.

Apparently, Marty was not a slow-start after all. Or, Mary brought him out of his shell. He seemed nicer to everyone these days. He took more time with me. He knew it was important to Nina. He spent time with Tommy playing basketball.

Nina and I had heard Angela telling him, "Work a solid ten hours a day and play a hard six hours. You will be happier – better at what you do."

It was true.

**Good times at Cumming Valley Farm.** Perhaps, Angela missed Duke too much. He was there as much as possible. He had many outstanding horses to watch over – all over the country.

Angela received twenty more two-year olds. This time Marty was doing most of the breaking. Mary was also helping. It was clear they were becoming a team. Mary's farm was being ignored other than the feeding of the animals. She wanted to be with Marty.

Angela was now more of a supervisor. Other than, she rode the trainees along with another exercise rider, who had come to the farm to help. There were now thirty-five horses in training – more than a full load.

"Your vacation is up, Tehachapi," Nina told me. "Back in the saddle you go."

Duke was home, so life was perfect. Angela was in heaven when her Duke was around. I had my Nina. Now Marty had Mary. What could be better?

"Let's see how much he's grown," said Duke to Nina, pulling out the measurer.

Duke, who stood six feet two inches tall, had no trouble transitioning the stick.

"He is fourteen-plus hands tall. I do not know if he is going to grow to fifteen hands. He may grow more when he gets to the track. I would guess he is going to be smaller than his daddy, No Rain."

"You think he's too small?"

"His daddy was the best horse racing of all time, in my book. Seabiscuit wasn't tall. Although, the Biscuit finish at 15.3 hands. I wish Tehachapi would finish out at fifteen hands. That is why I gave him the time. We'll see."

With that, I was back under tact.

"Gallup him, and galloped him and galloped him some more," Duke instructed.

For Nina and I, gallops were no problem. We love to go three, four and five miles. I was already in superb shape, because Nina had used me for a pony horse, as well as taking long gallops through Cummings Valley.

Time was fleeting. Once a week, Angela would ride me at a pretty good pace going a mile. Nina and I floated miles in between.

"Most horses would have crumbled," said Duke with a practiced eye. "He's teaching me something. I still don't believe."

Within four weeks, Duke was home again. He asked, "How far is Tehachapi ready to breeze?"

I looked at Angela, awaiting instruction.

"We've poured in long gallops. He's had some open breezes up to a mile," Angela answered. "Tehachapi is different than your ordinary horse racing. He's always been treated differently by Nina. I would say have her go three quarters in 1:13 or 14. When she gets there have her judge if he's tired or not."

Duke looked somewhat stern. Looking at Nina, he said, "I don't want you to press him. I do not want him to exhausted, trying to go too far. Understand?"

"I've learned breezing horses in twelve seconds an eighth of a mile; is that what you want?"

"Yes. My only concern is how far?"

"Tehachapi can go a mile in twelve seconds an eighth of a mile, and will be bucking two minutes after the work. We've put in a lot of miles together."

"Let's go three-quarters of a mile in 1:13 and just gallop him out another quarter."

"Will do," said Nina, backtracking away.

Nina and I went to the end of the track, and walked into the starting gate. Nina and I had practiced many times coming out of the gate, so it was no new mystery for me.

Duke nearly screamed, "I didn't mean to take him out of the gate three-quarters of a mile."

"Relax."

"You will be amazed. Nina is a natural. She actually comes out of the gate better than I do. She started at such an early age – it's no big deal. Bite your tongue, watch her."

"Okay. Whatever, you say, my love." He looked fondly at his wife.

"Tehachapi is no sprinter. His first quarter will be slower than twenty-four seconds."

"No problem. I'm not going to start him sprinting ever."

The bell sounded; the gate opened, and away we went. I was a slow learner out of the gate. However, now with Nina, I had confidence. That day, I used my smallish size to my advantage and was away quickly.

We were working with another horse, The Bart's Revenge, who powered into stride. At the eighth pole, Revenge was four lengths in front.

"What time do you have to the quarter-mile?" asked Duke.

"Timed Revenge in twenty-three and Tehachapi in twenty-four."

Duke said, "Have our new rider take some instructions from our nine-year-old." He was not kidding.

Revenge and Tehachapi worked to the half-mile, with Revenge still holding an easy lead. At the end of the half-mile, Tehachapi was a length behind. Down the stretch, coming to the end of the three-quarter, Nina let Tehachapi out just a notch.

"I've got the instruction," I told my little giant on my back. "I have been taught well by Angela. Out a notch means faster," I crowed.

I was not the slightest bit tired. I wondered when she was going to let me run. Nonetheless, 'out a notch', I would show them.

Duke said, "That bugger floats similar to his daddy, all four never touching."

My legs did touch, of course. I was so proficient at bounding away – your eyes had better focus quickly.

In the end, my time was 1:11 3/5ths, two lengths in front of the Revenge.

The Revenge had been working for a month. At the end of three quarters, his jockey shut him down. He was tired. Nina and I galloped out. We were having great fun "playing horse racing" and just getting our second wind.

"Easy boy," Nina instructed. "We don't want to get in trouble again. Just float along."

So float we did. Just an easy gallop, doing our 12s. At the end of a mile, Nina slowed us to a trot; ultimately, to a walk, as we cooled down.

Duke questioned, "Okay, tell me, how fast you guys went for a mile? I know you nudged him back at the end of three quarters."

"The final quarter after the wire in about twenty-four seconds – galloping," said Nina. "Tehachapi just floats."

"1:35 2/5ths."

"He has no speed, but he can go forever. He is one speed. Add all the quarters together, and at a distance, he's faster than any of the others here at the farm," Nina said.

I thought, "There are miracles. My legs do not creak. No more aches. And, now Nina says I'm the best."

Back at the barn, Duke asked, "Nina, were you asking him the last quarter?"

"No, we were just galloping. Having fun – as we do when we prance through the Valley."

# Chapter 12

**The Next Morning – the Great Debate.** In the early months of my life, no one wanted me. Everyone, except Nina, was certain I was a loser. This day – there was a debate.

"About me – gracious gander."

What is the next step? How could I become a "great" horse racing?

"I think we should ship him to the track, where Scrap can be certain he doesn't go too fast, too soon." Duke's assessment.

"This is his first work, here at the track. All the others have gotten at least four. Furthermore, Nina is here. He will continue to improve as long as Tehachapi is near her." Angela's assessment.

"Oh, I'm sure Tehachapi will be fine at the track. Nina and Tehachapi will improve." Marty Torres's assessment.

"I don't think Tehachapi should go to the track until either Angela, or I can be there. I think he will be great. I believe he has the greatest chance of being injured if we're not aboard him." Nina's words of advice.

In the end, Duke Snyder was the boss; Angela the conscience of the racing stable; and little Nina Torres – the one with the best assessment.

"Tehachapi will stay, until Angela returns to Hollywood Park to ride him," Duke's decision.

Angela had been working hard under Duke's instructions to get Marty Torres to the point he could take over. Angela was also working with both Torii and Nina, in breaking the two-year-olds.

Ultimately, Angela was going to split her time between Hollywood Park, Cummings Valley and taking trips with Duke on the road.

"I believe you'll be ready in a month," Angela told Marty. Moreover, she confided, "Duke and I are going to try to have a child. Once we do, I'm going to spend most of my time here. I'll be responsible for the horses on our training track, and leave the rest, including the breeding of No Rain to you."

Marty replied, "Hopefully, to Mary and me."

Thus was set the month of transition. It was summer once again, and I spent a great deal of the time with Nina and my new friend the warmblood. Every seven days I got to pick up my heels and work. Never again was I forced to work less than a mile.

"When I get to go racing once a week, I love it," I told my friend the warmblood. "There is nothing better. The wind goes through my mane, and the excitement in the air is breathtaking."

"Oh, you're such a geek," said Nina. "I remember the days you cried you were creaky and slow. Now you believe yourself to be a wonder horse. You still couldn't out sprint a snail," Nina replied.

"I don't race snails, or puppy-dog tails. Don't sprint, because that's for the faint of heart. My girl taught me to gallop long and gallop strong."

The warmblood told me, "You guys are such hams."

On my third work, which was set for 1.5 miles, the warmblood jumped out of the paddock and meandered to watch. I taught this big feller my ways of enjoying the farm. Before my instructions, he could not jump a lick without orders from Mary, but I made him understand we the mighty wander the farm.

Mary was beside herself; not understanding why the warmblood would jump from the paddock. However, as much as she tried to get him to move from viewing the track, she could not.

"Once his friend Tehachapi was finished, he just jogged to the paddock – jumped back in.

"The best I can figure he must miss Tehachapi when he's not in the paddock with him," said Mary.

Nina and I did not try to explain. We knew why the warmblood had jumped.

Angela and Nina were splitting the time breezing me. One time Angela would work me, and I would learn some new tricks. The next time Nina would be aboard doing the breeze.

Now that we were working 1.5 miles, and galloping out from there, it did make a difference having a 45-pound weight break.

"I'm not saying Angela is heavy, but Nina is no weight at all."

Occasionally, Angela would assign Torii to ride me.

"I want Tehachapi to get experience with other riders, because at the track, he will have jockeys guiding him in races. Torii weighed 126 pounds, and was heavy-handed compared to either Angela or Nina. She had a lot to learn.

Another change came when Mary and Marty decided to live together on the warmblood farm. Tommy and Nina would go with them after training hours, cutting my days short with my first love.

"I'm religious," I told Nina. "People who aren't married should not live together."

"You are just saying that. You're jealous."

"No, God told me. Get married. Then, live together. Not before."

They would leave my friend the warmblood in the stall next to me.

I did have someone to talk to, even if it was someone with a German accent.

**The Last Weekend.** Duke was home from winning five stakes races over the three days. It became commonplace for this young trainer to amass legendary wins across the land.

He scheduled works at the farm for Saturday morning.

"I'm to work a mile and 1/16, out of the gate," I told the warmblood.

I overheard Uncle Duke talking to my friend Angela.

"No advantage. You ride him, Angela. He will have to carry your weight," said Duke.

"Oh thanks. You're saying your wife is getting heavy?"

"No, you know that's not what I mean. I love your form. I think you are light from overwork – not heavy."

"You're right. I am down to 107 pounds. I need someone else doing the cooking," said Angela.

"Hope soon you are eating for two," said Duke, doting on his wife.

"Enough of that," said Mary. "You guys are disgusting."

Angela responded, "You don't have anything to talk about. You and my brother have become inseparable."

Mary beamed.

Angela has learned from Nina that I need warming up more than the usual thoroughbred. Whether the necessity came from my early months, I do not know. If I did not get enough warm-ups, I would take the time during the breeze. No floating before I was warm. A return to the slug stage.

She backtracked me three-quarters of a mile. Finally, she turned me around – took me to the gate.

"Why did she warm Tehachapi up so much?" asked Duke to Nina – taking notes. Many things made Duke Snyder an extraordinary trainer. Among the traits was studying identifying characteristics of each horse. He treated every animal distinctly different, depending upon what was needed.

Nina was on hand to explain, "Tehachapi is stiff. He was so little when he was born. He also was very thin and always cold. You have to warm him up until he floats. I cannot explain it, but a good rider can feel it. Once he is limber he tells you – he's ready to work."

Meanwhile, I went into the starting gate with another companion two- year-old – being ridden by Tori. When the gate opened, the large horse on the inside intentionally veered into me. I had my air knocked out, and I crashed off stride.

"Easy Tehachapi," said Angela steadying me. Now she was talking to me. Without her sure hands, we both would have fallen.

The other horse was off – way in front of us. Angela finally got us into stride.

"Easy, Tehachapi. We don't have to make it up all at once. We're going a distance today boy, so into your float; away we go," she said.

Nina and Duke saw the incident from the viewing stand. They saw I was knocked off my feet by the heavier animal.

"Oh, I hope he's okay," Nina pleaded.

Duke replied, "He's going to get worse when he is racing. So maybe, it is better we start with some incidents here on the farm. Let's see what he does under adversity."

I might not have been fast into stride, but soon I was floating over the ground. The lump of a horse in front of me might be a bully, but he was never going to make much of a horse racing.

I remember him from the paddock. He would bite; steal my food. Kick at me.

"Listen to who is talking now," I said to myself. "I might not be fast – I'm steady."

Soon Angela and I were in the clear; well beyond the fading horse. He was pulled up from his work. I was off alone flying around the half-mile track. I would see Duke watching. Nina and Mary cheering.

Angela's trained fingers told me to march on with a steady pace. A 16th from the end, she let me out two notches, and shook the reins at me.

"I've never heard this language, reins shaking, but I understood. Asked finally to do my best. She did not let me run much, before she pulled slightly on my mouth; full-out running was exhilarating.

"Watch him fly! I've never seen him move more beautifully," said Nina.

Duke's trained eyes saw Tehachapi's graceful movements; poetry to a trainer is time.

"1:45 2/5ths. Brilliant. Angela only worked him an eighth. His time could win a maiden claimer Hollywood, right now."

# Chapter 13

**A Plot Is Hatched.** "Good-bye Tehachapi," cried Nina.

I was loaded into the longest, biggest horse van I had ever seen. There were many other horses already tucked inside. Three of us from Cummings Valley Ranch departed that day for Hollywood Park to start our racing careers.

"Good-bye for now, my Nina. See you soon. I will do you proud by trying my best. I will try my best when I race, I promise," I told Nina in a voice crackling with a little fear.

I dreamt of going off to the races. I heard stories of the Great Race Place, Santa Anita. My mom, Ms. Mary, has told me of the good life with Scrap and Duke at Hollywood Park. Even so, new things are always frightening.

We did not talk much during the ride. I missed Nina already. Missed my friend the warmblood. I loathed Cummings Valley farm so much in the beginning.

I even miss the immense barn, which overpowers the landscape. Those cold and frigid mornings where Jack Frost creeps into your bones.

The little girl, with the iron brace, who limps in obvious pain, is a reminder that if "she" can find joy in the mornings, why cannot everyone.

"I feel the hand of God embracing my tiny feet – certainly my soul. I may be small, but my heart is mighty. God may have failed to grant me speed – he has promised me endurance. I had been born in the mountains, where my lungs grew large. A gift of more oxygen – whatever that means.

"Honestly, I do not know everything of which I speak. Much of it, I repeat as a litany, from what I've learned from Nina. However, the greatest power with which I've been imbued by the littlest Angel is a desire to do my best, to win."

The trip from Tehachapi to Hollywood Park took about two hours. In the end, I was happy to be leaving the bumpy horse van.

Moreover, my eyes were wide open as I entered the backside at Hollywood Park. The barns were made of cement blocks; as my mother had described. They were quite dissimilar to the metal structure I called home.

Inside, I learned that Duke Snyder had 78 spanking-new two-year-olds at the track. Cummings Valley farm was stocked with another 50 to 75 starter horses. It was plain to understand what Duke and Angela planned.

Duke intended to weed out the two-year-olds that could not perform. My life already taught me racing is about winners and losers. With about 22,000 thoroughbred babies born every year, the odds were long against being a champion or racing in the Kentucky Derby or the Preakness.

I already surpassed the expectations of all those who saw me grow up. Tyler and Catrina gave me away – certain I was not worth the tail of a donkey.

Duke intended to cull more extensively. He was given the best of the best. He intended to grow a stable to even greater heights. He had invested mightily in a large farm where he could stock hundreds of young horses.

Scrap came over as I was led into my stall.

"He's like his daddy. Lower the webbing or he will walk right under. I know this guy from Cummings Valley Ranch. He had the use of the farm. He walked the ranch unrestrained."

He bent and felt all four of my legs and feet. Bending was not easy for the 400-pound giant.

"I've heard stories of how fast he's worked, and how far he has gone. I'm surprised, he has any legs left. However, there is not a bump. He is the epitome of health. He is smaller than his daddy. His eye has the same keenness." Scrap's assessment.

Scrap added quietly, "Move him to stall four. I'll rub him myself."

Where others had measured me, Scrap did not. He made his assessment based on instinct and a half-century of experience. There was an immediate kinship.

Duke and Scrap assigned Angela to ride the best fifteen of the young horses. I was one of her charges. I had the best – Scrap and Angela.

"How could I lose?"

Could tell you of all the little things I learned, but I will stick to the highlights. The training stable was much more intense than the farm. A groom had the responsibility for three or four horses with Scrap overseeing them. Duke, of course, was the headmaster.

Scrap rubbed the first four horses, including me. He had an assistant groom, Mr. Brown – who helped him. Mr. Brown seemed as if he was 150 years old. Both Scrap and Mr. Brown moved extremely slowly; however, they were meticulous. With two of them overlooking me, my slightest ache was discovered. Before I even realized I had pain.

Mr. Brown introduced me to a new type of blanket. He would put it over my back once or twice a week. It was warm and heated me. It also seemed to soothe spots, which had become tired or worn from working.

I worked harder now. Nina and I always galloped long. There was no change. Angela was trying something new with me. I would gallop two or three miles one day at a good pace. Then, I would return the next day – gallop a mile faster than normal – but not breezing – galloping out.

"You'll kill him," Scrap cried. "Give him a break. No horse can do that."

"Not so sure," said Duke.

Angela would say, "He's bucking and playing when I take him off the track."

I never really ran out of gas. On our fast mile gallops, I certainly felt extended, when Angela would take me another mile.

"It was fun." I would tell my Nina.

The first couple of weeks I did not breeze. I had my new work pattern. Put in the miles. Every afternoon, Scrap and Duke would methodically check my legs and feet.

"It seems he's impervious to the normal ailments that adversely affect horse racings. His tendons are tight and cool. If we worked the traditional horse as we do him, the thoroughbred's legs would fall off," Duke said.

I learned some racing history from what they were trying with me. Over the past century, thoroughbreds had become more brittle. Owners were looking for speed. Wanted the fastest horse alive. Not the best. Forget the classic distance.

"They sacrificed stamina," said Duke.

"Yes, they bred distance out of our modern-day horses. In the years before, thoroughbreds could race a 100 times. Now many times the champion horse racing will retire with only ten or fifteen starts— maybe less," said Mr. Brown, the old man at the barn.

Duke agreed, "Look at No Rainbows. He was extremely fast; pounded the ground. He retired after nineteen starts, winning every race unless he ran against No Rain. He is now breeding stake's winner after champion. However, they will not have ultimate soundness or stamina."

Angela asked, "Surely, we're not going to work him to death, and never breeze him? Are we?"

"No. You will take him on one faster gallop, a mile and a half this time. I'll pony him for three days. After a day off, we'll have him work a mile," Duke instructed.

Scrap said, "Why don't you have jockey Joe Calamos race him instead of working him? He'd be 100 to one as small as he is."

"Good idea, Scrap. Nonetheless, we have to have three registered works in order to enter. Why don't we break him off breezing a mile, but ask for a four furlong recorded work?" Duke responded.

Angela said, "He goes so evenly – not fast – that no one would consider him to be working a mile. I can start from the wire in an extended gallop, and work him four furlongs."

With the strategy conspired, I was sent on the path. Day one: Angela and I moved quickly and astutely through an extended gallop for mile and a half.

Duke was called on the carpet by the stewards, who inquired what he was doing.

"You can't work horses; and not have the time recorded," warned the steward.

"I wasn't working him. He just gallops fast and long. I am trying to train him."

Everyone knew Duke was up to something. No one knew what.

On the seventh day, my legs were wrapped, and I went to the track. Unusually, Scrap and Mr. Brown and a boatload of others from the barn came out to watch Angela breeze me.

I was to start out working quarters in twenty-four seconds, as Nina called it "the magical 12s." Another two-year-old, who was a sprinter, would break off with me and work four furlongs.

At the wire, Angela said, "Here we go. Nice and easy. Long strides, Tehachapi." I began floating. I was delighting in bounding from one take off to another.

"I have him in forty-seven seconds and change for the first half," said Duke to his friend and companion attorney Cory Bentley. They were watching from the kitchen balcony, as the two of them normally did.

"You are going to get your goose cooked over this work," predicted Cory.

"Don't think so," said Duke. "When the two-year-old Bart colt beats him to the wire, everyone will dismiss Tehachapi."

The Bart colt was a large and buff two-year-old, who was ready to race. He had worked easily seven days before. Duke and Cory picked the Dovato two-year-old to win his first start. Therefore, they believed he could easily handle Tehachapi, who had already galloped fast for half-mile.

"Here we go boy. Stay up the best you can," said Angela.

"I'll give you all that I have," I promised her. I knew she could not understand my words, but would see my actions.

I was on the rail, with the Bart colt on my outside. Pressing into me.

"Get off of me," ordered Angela. "You're going to push us over the rail."

"I've been instructed not to give the little guy any breaks," said jockey Joe Calamos. "The boss man has instructed me to kick your butt."

"If you kill me, Duke will have your head," screamed Angela.

As the two of them bantered, the Bart colt pressed quickly through the first quarter. He was fresh and fast. I did my best; nonetheless, found myself two lengths behind at the end of the first quarter.

Calamos guided the Bart colt over onto the rail blocking any notion Angela had of coming up the shortest distance. Calamos had been on the losing end when No Rain had defeated No Rainbows. He did not know how fast Tehachapi was. He, however, respected the legacy of No Rain.

When we headed into the stretch, Angela shook the reins at me. I had now learned her signal with delight. We had gone a distance, I knew, but candidly, I was not tired. My lungs filled with air. Since we had come to lower elevation, it seems as if there was so much to breathe.

"Okay, Tehachapi, show me what you have," said Angela.

I flew. I moved over the ground as No Rain had done before. No one measured my stride that day – but it was long.

"Up to your old tricks, are you?" Calamos asked as we caught him.

I had the momentum, but Calamos was sitting on dynamite. He shook the reins at the Bart colt, which put me away, pulling two – then three lengths – in front by the time the wire came.

"How did you like that?" kidded Calamos.

"He's fast. Faster than this little guy."

Calamos had a surprised expression on his face. He did not understand why he was asked to work the Bart colt against such a little tyke. That was not No Rain. What is the idea?

"How fast did you get them working a half mile?" Cory asked.

Duke responded, "I have Tehachapi in 45 and change."

"That's a crazy 1:32 for the mile," exclaimed Cory. "Impossible."

"Until today, I would have agreed with you. I'll bet you when we get to the barn Tehachapi won't even take a drink of water," Duke bragged.

"Perhaps, you have found the secret on how to train No Rain's colts. They're Energizer bunnies – they go, and go and go."

Duke was correct. When they got back to the barn, I was not blowing at all from the work. I was disappointed the braggart colt had cleaned my clock. He was bragging to every horse in the barn that would listen that Nina's favorite was "still slow as a snail."

He certainly was faster. Let me see him go around two turns.

"I thought the little guy would get him," said Scrap.

"Asking too much, with the Bart colt only working a half. I think up to seven-eighths of a mile the Bart colt will prevail. After that, there will be no contest," Duke explained.

Joe Calamos approached Duke.

"What's the idea of having that little guy tackle my robust mount? Totally unfair to the tyke."

"I guess, I lost my mind."

Calamos knew Duke Snyder did not do irrelevant things. He understood Duke was not prone to miscalculations. However, he certainly had no idea of the plot hatched by the trainer. Why he was instructed to give Angela's mount a tough time?

The answer would come another day.

# Chapter 14

**Almost Calamity at the Start.** Seven days later, Joe Calamos was given the riding instructions on Tehachapi.

Duke said, "Take him out of the gate and work him five furlongs. Let him gallop out another mile."

"What?"

"Didn't understand?"

"I'm to gallop him out a mile after working him five furlongs."

"Exactly. Do the five furlongs about a minute and change."

"I don't understand. You worked this guy strangely last week, and what we're doing this week seems bizarre."

Joe Calamos worked all of Duke's horses that he was going to ride. Calamos was not even certain he wanted this mount. Tehachapi was significantly smaller than No Rain. He had not seen anything to impress him.

"What's the idea?" asked Calamos' agent.

"You guys don't want the mount?"

"Joe has three more to work this morning. It appears this young-fellow needs many more works, before he races. Certainly, before he wins.

"Okay Joe, climb down," instructed Duke.

Calamos sat frozen for a moment, and, then, he followed instructions. He got down off Tehachapi. He shook Duke's hand. Thanked him for the two horses he had worked earlier that morning.

Duke looked in the directory of his cell phone – finding the number for Nettie Brierley. She had second call on Duke's young horses. Nettie had recently married another jockey, who normally raced in Canada. They were giving the Southern California circuit a chance before returning to a northern track. Both understood racing locally for them was a long shot.

Duke started riding Nettie because his former owners Bob and Mary Mays always gave young females a chance. They owned No Rain and No Rainbows, as well as Tehachapi's mother Ms. Mary.

Nettie had been loyal, and Duke had returned the favor. Nettie did not have the arm strength of Calamos. She was weaker down the stretch; nonetheless, horses were keen for her finesse and kindness. They ran for her.

"Nettie, I hope you are still here at the Park. You worked a couple for me earlier today. I have one more for you to get on. You can ride him to victory when he goes."

"I'll be right over!"

Nettie, blonde-haired, blue-eyed lass, was tall and skinny with small breasts. She resembled a boy – reminded Tehachapi of his Nina.

She jogged enthusiastically into the barn. "What's up?"

"I want you to work Tehachapi five furlongs from the gate, and gallop him out another mile," Duke said, repeating the instructions.

"Five from the gate, gallop him out a mile."

"Exactly."

Nettie was lifted on Tehachapi's back.

"He's little."

Angela, who had been standing quietly through the jockey ordeal, moved up to Nettie, as she walked Tehachapi away from Duke.

"He's small, but you will like him.  Be sure to warm him up a good half mile before the work.  Did you get a split-time from Duke?"

"No.  I know Duke wants slow.  I would assume one and change."

Angela yelled to Duke, "How fast?"

"One minute."

Nettie nodded.

Nettie Brierley is special.  She is kindhearted, and showed it as she straightened my mane, and patted me tenderly on my neck.

"What's your story boy?  I could tell Angela loves you.  She was standing right on top of me, mothering you," said Nettie.

She warmed me intuitively by backtracking a half mile. Turning, she took me in the starting gate, and when the bell rang and the doors sprung open, I shot forward.  I almost unseated her, as she did not expect me to react so quickly.  One of her feet slipped out of the irons; she—momentarily – lost her balance.

We struggled forward for the first quarter a mile, as Nettie regained her irons and balance.  We worked the 5/8s of a mile in a slow time of 1:03 4/5ths, and continued our gallop.  Nettie's hands told me she wanted me to slow the gallop for the mile. I was floating along, enjoying my task.

When we got back to the barn, I tried to tell Nettie I enjoyed my time with her.  She could not understand me the way my Nina did.  She was very kind, petting me softly on my muzzle. Nettie was very jittery, because she understood her failure to complete the task as instructed.

"Tehachapi was so quick into stride, I lost my stirrup. My loss of balance affected our time. I hope I get another chance on him. Once I understood how he moves, I very much enjoyed him. He may be a shorty, but he has an incredible stride. Has anyone measured it?"

Angela said, "Yes, he does move away from the gate rather quickly. Tehachapi is not fast. Any horse in the barn can beat him for a quarter, but there is none here that will match him for a mile – remember that. He is steady. He never quits."

Duke ambled back into the barn. "Lost your stirrup, huh?"

"Yep, got him now."

"That's why we have the jockey who is going to ride a particular horse work him a time or two. Let's set him up to work back in five days. Then, he'll be ready to go."

"Great."

You could see the relief in Nettie's eyes when Duke forgave her for missing the start. It was obvious; Nettie had been beaten up trying to become a race jockey. She fit with Nina and me.

Duke thought it was much easier working with Nettie Brierley, rather than Joe Calamos. She was not a natural in the saddle. She did not have Joe's innate instincts, or his strength. In a match race, Calamos would win ten out of ten times.

"However, on Tehachapi Nettie Brierley might be the right cup of coffee. He had always performed with Nina and Angela. Let's keep it simple."

# Chapter 15

**Still Unappreciated.** Nettie returned days later, and Tehachapi and Nettie worked six furlongs, galloping another mile. Duke instructed Nettie to work slow and steady – treating the entire mile and three quarters as the same work. I had slogged through the six furlongs with her holding me every step, and galloped freely for another mile.

"Good job Nettie. Duke said, "He's ready to rumble."

Nettie had a concerned expression when she asked, "How far? What distance will we race?"

Duke immediately understood her concern. Decided to have some fun at her expense.

"I was thinking five furlongs; what do you think?"

"I'll do whatever you ask. I have concern he may not be fast enough," she muttered, with her eyes focused on the ground.

"How far would you race him? And what company do you think he fits in?"

Nettie looked up.

"Mr. Duke, I think he has to go around two turns. I certainly would run him in a claiming race to start. He's so small, no one will claim him. In that class, around two turns, I think he has a good chance."

Days later, it was the big day for me — race day. My dad had won consecutively; in fact, never lost. Beat the best-of-the-best.

"Talk about pressure," I thought.

Certainly, no one expected a record performance out of me. I wanted to enjoy my freedom while racing today, instead of restrained. I needed to keep my promise to Nina to give my all.

The Daily Racing Form analyzed my three works. They reported the moves were slow – nothing special. Additionally, they reported, "No Rain offspring had never won first time out."

Furthermore, No Rain, as a sire, did not produce a single colt able to break his maiden at the highest level. Even low claimers fared poorly. They picked me to come in last.

"What's more, what is Duke Snyder thinking about racing this first-time starter against winners? And these are more than winners – the best stakes' horses on the grounds."

**Things as usual.** I'm the loser colt – out of the loser stallion. Too small, too slow.

"I've heard it a thousand times before," I thought.

I would have cried, if I had not promised to try my best.

"Back again into the mire. Everyone looks at my size, and considers my dad a no account. I'm going to prove them wrong."

Nettie Brierley was winning seven percent of her races, but when mounting Duke's horses she won at a twenty-two percent clip. The racing form said, "Joe Calamos is Duke Snyder's number one call, with Nettie Brierley mopping up from a strong barn."

I did not even have the best rider. However, if I could not have Nina or Angela, I wanted Nettie Brierley. She was kind, always warmed me up before we started racing.

This racing business is all new to me. To be honest, a bit scary. I was taken in the morning to some barn where the stewards checked my lip to see if my racing number matched my racing papers.

"One look at me should have told them who I was," I thought sarcastically.

I saddled in another location by Duke and Scrap. It was almost too much.

Finally, I was delighted to see Nina standing in the mounting enclosure. I learned Nina had flown in with Duke and Angela that morning.

"You must fly yourself today — Tehachapi. For both of us. This is our race. We have a lot to prove," said Nina as she hugged me around the neck.

A steward came over to Duke.

"That little girl with a brace on is going to get hurt. It is your responsibility to watch her," he instructed.

"She raised him. If she were old enough, I would ride her today. Tehachapi would lie down and roll over like a dog, if she told him. She is at no risk."

Mary, who also came. She moved over and put her hand softly on Nina's shoulder. Angela observed Mary. Was happy to see the two had bonded. It was as if Mary was now Nina's mom.

"I pray Nina doesn't get hurt. The divorce almost killed her," Angela said to herself, closing her eyes for a second in a silent prayer.

Nina embraced Tehachapi softly again. Moved back several steps with Mary.

Duke introduced Nettie to Nina, and told her the little girl was responsible for the colt being at the track today.

"He's wonderful," Nettie said.

"Nina, what instructions would you give?"

Nina, looking at her Tehachapi with pride, said candidly, "He is not the fastest, but he has more heart than all of them put together. Tehachapi will not quit."

"Okay"

Nina continued, "Get out of the gate and find an opening. Don't get him knocked off of his feet. Get him in an open space. Let him have his head."

Angela, who is standing only a stride away, said, "When you get to the quarter pole, shake the reins at him. Be sure he has open ground because the others will be tiring. He will not."

Duke waited patiently. "Keep him six or so off the lead. He can go in and out of horses. Angela is correct, when you get a quarter-mile from home, shake the reins and sit chilly."

Nettie said, "You guys sound as if it's going to be a cake-walk. There are some very good horses in here, including five winners. Braveheart has never lost."

"Remember, how I told you that you were sitting on the best horse when you raced No Rain?" encouraged Duke. "Well, Ditto!"

"I've got it."

"Don't fall off," Duke said with a smile.

Nettie and Tehachapi circled the walking enclosure once, and headed on to the Hollywood Park oval.

Duke Snyder was a trainer – not a gambler. However, his bet on No Rain was legendary. He had bet—won—and gave the winning ticket to his groom, Scrap.

Today, Duke hoped to outdo that story.

Duke put $3,000 to win on Tehachapi, when the betting opened. He did it in several small bets, so no one would see it all plunked down at one time.

After he left the saddling enclosure, he gave Angela another $5,000 to bet on Tehachapi. This was a stakes race, and a lot of money was being bet by big-time owners.

He also got a $1,000 trifecta, picking the order of the first three finishers – naturally, putting Tehachapi on top, Braveheart second, and the entire field to come in third. If his first two horses finished one-two, Duke could not lose.

There were twelve starters today in the first event for two-year-olds at mile and a sixteenth.

This was a $150,000 stakes race. This first event around two turns for two-year-olds this year. Five horses had cost their owners more than a million dollars.

Tehachapi had only $8,120 bet on him to win — almost all of it bets by Duke. This was no surprise, because everyone knocked the too-small colt.

Furthermore, when the betting public got a chance to see him, they were shocked. He looked like a kid's pony. When the race started, Tehachapi's odds were $43 to 1.

Nettie rested comfortably on top of Tehachapi in the gate. Joe Calamos was two enclosures away on one of the favorites to win. Calamos' mount had won twice, including a stake's race at six furlongs in 1:09, which was fast for young horses.

Duke had elected to start Tehachapi at a mile and a sixteenth, because he knew his horse needed distance. He did not fear the other horses when they were going this route of ground.

The distance also suited Calamos' mount. He was by a stake's winner of eleven races, including winning the prestigious Preakness and Breeders Cup. The horse cost $4.6 million dollars as a yearling.

The Daily Racing Form already anointed him the winner of this event, and one of the favorites for next year's Triple Crown events.

Duke and Angela were watching the race from a TV monitor, with Angela a stride to Duke's left.

"Get him away clean," Angela said in a silent prayer.

The announcer high in the stands called the race. The horses thundered away from the starting gate.

"There they go."

As usual, Tehachapi jettisoned away a step in front of the others, even the sprinters. He was not fast, but he was quick from the gate. It allowed Nettie to get a position without being bumped.

"Around the first turn, it's Calamos aboard Braveheart by two lengths."

Nettie had done a good job tucking Tehachapi in at the rail, but keeping him slightly off, so no one could crowd the small colt.

"He's moving as his father," Duke said with pride. Nettie's got him in a good position four from the front, saving all the ground."

I was not moving with any haste, but was enjoying myself with this bunch. Into the backstretch, I moved up into third about three lengths behind Braveheart. He was moving powerfully. I felt good gliding along.

Nettie did something unexpected when we were three-eighths of a mile from home. She let my reins out a notch, which told me to move a little. I did not expect her to let me move so quickly.

The announcer saw us on-the-go, and reported, "Tehachapi has now caught Braveheart – they are head-and-head. They are three-eighths of a mile from the finish."

Joe Calamos was positive Braveheart could put away the little runt, so he did not panic. He snafued this little tyke in a work on a lesser horse. He had his tall and mighty steed on the rail. Little Tehachapi moved to the outside.

"Go wide with your nag," he yelled at Nettie.

She said nothing.

The two horses raced together around the turn. No one from the grandstand could see Tehachapi.

"He's so small — did he disappear dad? Questioned a small boy.

I was dwarfed by Braveheart. Joe Calamos let his mount out and shook the reins at him. Braveheart held us at bay, but was unable to pull away.

At the top of the stretch, Nettie looked at Joel Calamos and said, "I'll see you."

She shook the reins at me. Frankly, I could not understand why she had not done it earlier. I was moving with ease with this other horse. I saw no reason not to have passed him some time ago.

Now, I was free. I was given my head. Nettie never cocked her whip. Even so, again, she urged me with her reins.

"Tehachapi has flown clear of Braveheart."

The crowd gasps in disbelief.

"He's moving like a winner. He is now six in front of Braveheart, and thirteen or fourteen lengths in front of the third-place finisher."

Nettie did me a favor and let me gallop out until we reached deep into the backside. I could have gone around again.

Duke cashed more than $125,000 in tickets that afternoon, plus the winner's share of the prize money.

"Nice ride. Why did you play with Calamos around the turn?"

"I wanted to be sure to win. I did not want to be cocky. I did not want to find myself in deep stretch against a horse that had already won a stake's race and find myself with a tired horse under me. I just waited until I was certain Braveheart was done."

Duke said, "Tehachapi is the only two-year-old horse on the ground that is ready to go more than a mile. They would beat him sprinting, but over a mile – forget it."

In the winner's circle, Nina was handed the lead rope, holding Tehachapi. Like my father, No Rain, I stood quietly. Maybe, I am more of a ham than dad is, because I posed for the pictures.

"Take a bunch," said Duke. "I want plenty to choose from."

For one, I nuzzled right up to my girl, Nina. I put my head down, and she threw her arms around me. We both looked directly at the camera.

As Nettie jumped down, Duke extended his hand to shake. Instead, the lovely young jockey hugged the trainer, because she was so grateful for the opportunity. She recognized the special talents of Tehachapi.

When the bright-eyed lass gave up the hug, and started to move away, Duke said, "You will want to shake my hand – as well."

Nettie looked confused, but took the trainers large mitt. Duke's hand dwarfed Nettie's. Completing the shake, the rider found two winning tickets tucked in her hand.

Moving away, she looked. Two, $100 win tickets. She gasped, because she knew the odds. Duke had just handed her tickets worth $8,600, plus the jockey's share of the purse worth more than $12,000. For a little more than a minute's work Nettie had earned $20,000.

Tears came into her eyes. Life had been difficult for her. Money ran out every-day – buying food even a problem. Of course, Duke was well aware. Nettie and her husband were on the last leg, thinking of jumping ship and heading to Canada. There, his father had a farm where they could live as they raced locally.

Nettie stopped frozen. Could not move. Then, she turned and half walked and half ran back to the tall man, who just saved her life.

She threw her arms around Duke's shoulder and gave him a kiss on the cheek.

"Thank you." After, she moved away crying.

Angela strolled over to her husband. "Have an admirer? Do you?"

"You know what 'we' did. It was your idea after all," said Duke.

"Yes. But you got the kiss."

# Chapter 16

**Evil Strikes Cummings Valley.** Two days after the winning race, Angela had received and urgent call. Angela was agitated when she left the phone. Almost nothing could stir up the mild-mannered brown-eyed rider, who caught her man when she patiently waited and ultimately married Duke.

They had never had a fight in the barn. Angela would bide her time. When they were alone, she would ease Duke into submission. A loving unity.

Today was different. This was clear when Angela left the phone.

"Duke," Angela said sternly, "I must take Tehachapi, and trailer him to the farm. Now, no-fuss – no-debate."

Nina's mother descended on the ranch in a maniacal rage — barely holding onto sanity.

Angela said, "The witch is taking over at Cummings Valley Ranch. It is going to destroy Marty and Mary. What's more, it is going to crucify those kids. It almost killed Nina when her mom walked out the first time."

Duke responded quietly, trying to pacify Angela, "Honey. I understand. Really, I do. I will fly you up there right after training hours today. We cannot take Tehachapi. He may be our best distant horse."

Angela nearly yelled. She caught herself.

"Some things are much more important than horses. Duke, you know I love you. You also know I have supported you every step as you grew the barn out of proportion. However, Nina needs Tehachapi. Her needs are more important than one horse."

Duke had never seen Angela inconsolable. He knew her heart. He knew family was first.

Tehachapi thought, "Obviously, I'm merely a horse — the subject of the conversation. I do not understand what is going on. I don't have my Nina to explain the spat to me.

"I certainly do not know a 'witch,' I said to myself. "Perhaps, I am about to meet one. Does she fly with a broomstick? Wear black clothing, and make death potions."

What I did understand, evil had fallen on Cummings Valley Ranch.

Angela, her hands and arms shaking, said, "I'm taking our Ford 350, and the two-horse trailer. I'd appreciate your help loading Tehachapi and seeing me off."

"If you won't, I am going anyway," said Angela, with her hands on her hips and her boots firmly planted.

Duke was anything, but a fool. Ultimately, she was the most important thing in his life – even if he did not show it sometimes.

"You are right," he said intelligently – understanding he had lost the battle.

He moved to her; took Angela in his arms, squeezing her against him. He looked down and kissed her on the forehead. On the bridge of her nose. In the end, he kissed her hard, as they forgot they had onlookers.

"I can get someone else to drive Tehachapi to the farm. If you want to wait until after training, I will fly both of us up to Cummings Valley Ranch."

Angela looked briefly at her watch, seeing it was only seven a.m. She decided to drive.

"I can be there by 8:30. Nina and Tommy are not in school. Because of the shenanigans, Mary has kicked all of them out. That forces Marty and the family back to the nutcase."

She continued, "I need to get to the ranch. By the time we fly up there it will be the afternoon."

Duke held her.

"You drive extremely slowly. You are precious cargo. I can't replace you. You are upset. I don't want you taking it out on the road. Won't help the kids if you get an accident."

The trainer called to Scrap, asking him to wrap Tehachapi's legs for transport. Duke went for the Ford and the trailer.

"In all the time I've known her, I have never seen her so unnerved," Duke thought. "She's the one who is rock solid."

He got the truck, hooked the trailer securely.

Angela kissed Duke apologetically. "Sorry hubby – you haven't done anything wrong. You don't deserve my ire."

"I understand. I love you. I will be up later. Make me the bad bloke, because I will kick some butt when I get there. You plan staying at the ranch for a while—let's get our kid-making machine underway. I want a family too. I want you to wrap all of us in your arms."

With a final kiss from Duke, Angela and I were on our way back to Cummings Valley Ranch. I sensed her depression. I wished I could ride with her, instead of in the trailer.

Time went quickly. Angela took her vengeance out on the road, with me bumping along behind.

Immediately, upon pulling into our ranch, I could feel how despondent everyone was – horses and all. People think animals don't understand when humans feel pain and anguish. Quite, the opposite is true.

Our thoroughbreds and the warmblood knew something was amiss. They did not understand exactly what had gone awry. Even so, they knew there was a devil present.

Marty and Tommy came out to meet the trailer. Both walked slowly with their heads down. Neither talked. Nina was nowhere to be seen.

I saw a slim woman with long brown hair come marching out of the barn—in command. To some, they would say she is pretty.

She wore a dress far too fancy for work in a racing barn. When she got close, her face was made up with deep, dark eye shadow — a monster. The reddest lipstick I ever saw.

"The witch," I thought.

She spoke with a sledge hammer. No softness — words as hard as concrete.

"Marty, get the kids. We're going into town for breakfast," she ordered.

It was 9:30 – far too late for breakfast on a horse ranch. It was evident she had gotten around not long before.

"Marty did you hear me?" she yelled.

Angela climbed out of the truck, giving her brother and Tommy a hug.

"Oh, isn't this sweet," said the lady with poison. "The buffoon is back. I'm sure everything will be alright now."

She didn't address Angela. And Angela said nothing to her. They obviously were not the best chums.

"Marty, will you give me a hand unloading Tehachapi. I brought him home for Nina. I thought it might help her."

He moved to unlatch the back of the trailer. The witch, who no one had called by name, said, "Don't give my husband instructions. I'll tell him what to do."

Angela said nothing.

Marty continued unloading.

"Tommy, go find your sister. Tell her Tehachapi is home. Tell her to come and take care of him. I can't merely turn a horse in training out in the open field," Marty instructed.

The boy was only too happy to be freed from the adults. He ran off to the recesses of the ranch to locate Nina.

"I'm going to our house to get our car, so we can go to breakfast. I'll return in five minutes – be ready."

Now that Angela and Marty were left alone, I saw Marty relax somewhat. Both were leading me to a stall inside the barn. They talked as they walked.

"I don't understand. What brought her back after all of this time?"

Marty answered, "She learned that I am living with Mary. The kids have a life. She does not want me – she does not want someone else to have me. She certainly doesn't want me to have a life and be happy."

I eavesdropped, as the two talked.

Angela said softly, "I don't know how a mother can hate her kids so much she would want to deny them."

I learned that no one ever called the lady by name – not Marty, not the children, and certainly not Angela.

"Why don't you demand she leave?"

"That's exactly what Mary demanded to know," said Marty. "That's why she threw me out."

"I don't blame her. I would have thrown your butt out too, if you are not man enough to stand up to the bitch," she said.

Angela was perhaps the kindness person alive. When it came to Marty's former wife, she had long ago lost patience.

Marty replied, "When we separated the final time, she took a baseball bat to me. Last night when we started to go around, she flew at me," said Marty – pointing to a deep gash on the side of his face and neck. "I can't expose my children to the insanity."

"What's the answer?"

Marty shrugged. "Most of all, I have to protect the children."

Angela could not disagree. She witnessed the woman fly off crazily. Marty and their brother had to pull the crazy loon off Angela's mother. Had they not been present, she would have killed their mom.

"Are you going with her to breakfast?"

"We'll have a scene if I don't. She's going to push everything to the hilt, especially now that you're here," said Marty. "I'll see if I can go alone. I'll try to keep the kids away from her."

"Does she know where Mary lives?"

"No, not exactly. She only knows Mary lives somewhere in the Valley."

Angela offered, "I'm going to try to get the kids and go see Mary. I will try being an icebreaker by explaining what you are up against. I will see if Mary is willing to have the children stay, while we sort this out."

"She will go crazy if she believes the children are with Mary."

"Well, don't tell her. You do have sole custody, right?"

"Yes. However, official orders do little when she starts striking. She is that gone. Before she was nuts. Now, she is on alcohol plus plenty of drugs. I don't know where she will stop."

"We must take baby steps," said Angela. "Protect the kids."

Marty said, "Maybe, it's best to have Nina take Tehachapi on a ride, and take Tommy along on his horse. Tell them to stay away until dark. Hopefully, by dark, we can come up with some sort of a plan."

"Sure, if you think that best."

The former wife returned driving a newish Mercedes sports car. She was back before Nina, and Tommy came.

"Where are the children?" she demanded.

"I don't know. You saw Tommy run off looking for his sister. They haven't returned."

That seemed to satisfy her.

"Well, I'm hungry. They will just have to miss breakfast."

The children ate hours earlier. Life on a horse ranch started early – she had no clue; even though she had lived there and ran off with the farm manager – who she jilted not long after.

Marty acquiesced. He got in the sports car, and she flew out of the ranch – far too fast for a working farm with children at play.

Immediately, after her departure, it was as if a cloud lifted from the ranch. The workers, and even the horses, seemed to understand that evil was gone. The devil was driving away.

At least for now.

# Chapter 17

**The Black Widow.** Angela called a meeting; she instructed the farm workers to walk all the training horses that had not been out.

"All the other horses do their normal routine. We'll see if we can get back to work in the morning."

At that moment, Angela saw Tommy running toward the barn, with his sister moving as quickly as she could with one good leg. One did not bend.

"Where is Tehachapi?" Nina asked.

"He is in his permanent stall."

Nina had painted Tehachapi's name on his stall door when she first put him there months before.  No one had guts enough to remove his name when Tehachapi was shipped to the track. His was the only stall that remained unused when he was away.

At first, Nina would check daily to see if any adult had removed his name. See if any skullduggery went on during her school time. She was ready with a paint brush to put "Tehachapi's" name back on the stall.

"Guard it, if necessary," she thought.

Without a word, Nina was off. Sprinting. Or, at least, running as fast as she could with her brace leg. Angela had to trail behind because Nina – even with an iron brace – moved quickly when it came to seeing her beloved Tehachapi.

"Give him a quick brush.  Check his legs.  Throw on a Western saddle, and take him for a slow gallop with your brother through Cummings Valley," said Angela.

Nina heard the firmness in her aunt's voice.

"Sure."

"Remember, Tehachapi is very sound now. He has had a winning race a few days ago at the track. He may run off with you, if you don't keep a close eye on him."

"I'll watch him. Tehachapi isn't going to run off," she said lovingly. "Not with me."

How grown-up, Angela thought, "She is only nine-years-old."

She lost a good part of her youth because of the circumstances surrounding her mother. Abandonment – throw-a-ways – death to a child.

Angela knew Tehachapi would help rekindle the love her mother was trying to drive a nail through the deserted child.

Within a few minutes, Angela saw Tommy and Nina leaving through the front gate. Nina would have to ride slower, because Tommy was not as adroit in the saddle. He might be years older, but she was ten years better.

**A Field Trip.** Angela was certain the children would not return for hours.

"Nina has her Tehachapi. Even with her brother along, it's a love affair. It will be all day. Didn't have to tell her to stay out until dark – it is routine when she is with her Tehachapi."

She knew Tommy and Nina had no love for the woman who had only abused them. Since the farm was effectively shut down for the day, Angela decided to visit Mary.

Angela's heart and softness returned as she drove into the hills above Bear Valley. Winter or summer, this place was touched by God. Its majesty transformed from season to season, but the splendor never rested.

"I know it's none of my business," she told Mary on her arrival. "On the other hand, I'm sure my brother has ineffectively explained what kind of danger the lady presents."

For the first five seconds, Mary was standoffish. Moments later, she threw her arms around Angela – broke into tears.

"I kicked your brother's behind off my farm," she explained. "He can't sleep with me and her too. He can't be in my bed, and, then, go home and sleep with her," Mary cried.

Angela said, "I need to explain the facts of life, and the birds and the bees to you about him."

The ladies walked slowly out onto Mary's 20-acre ranchet. The little farm was manicured – perhaps, a little too neat for a working ranch. It certainly had the woman's touch, with green grass walkways, and flowers plentiful. In the highlands, flowers would die as seasons changed; however, Mary would immediately plant new ones, which were in bloom.

Mary had two barns. One barn housed her warmblood stallion, and in the other, she had mares, and a foaling stall. She also had a large arena with different size jumps. Additionally, there was a starting area, where the young horses were trained over fences.

Over the next two hours, the women chatted and worked with the warmbloods. Angela told Mary about a proud man, who had tried to protect his two children from a woman obsessed with money, sex, drugs and everything wild. With evil.

"Most guys would have knocked her out. My brother to his credit kept his hands in his pockets."

Mary took in Angela's words; in fact, ate them as if starving for information – trying to reconnect with Marty. Mary insisted that Angela mount one her trained jumpers who regularly did the professional circuit.

For the first time in a number of years, Angela was delighted to ride and jump. By the end of the afternoon, she had taken one of the better jumping four-year-olds over a five-foot fence. She sat chilly – no bobble. She hit the takeoff spot perfectly, sending the horse skyward.

"This brings back fond memories. I had to sell my jumper when my dad died in order to settle his estate. I went off to the track, and fell in love with the love of my life."

Mary giggled. They both were 16 again.

"My man is at your farm. He should walk away from the witch. She can sleep in his bed — alone."

By the end of the afternoon, the ladies walked as sisters, with Mary agreeing she would give Marty a chance to square the relationship.

"He's still must rid himself of her before he can come back here."

"I couldn't agree more. However, Marty won't do anything to endanger the children, so it may take a while. Soon, she will bore of him and take off. That is a short-term solution. What you guys are going to do long-term, I don't know."

Angela's cell phone played a tune, which told her the farm was calling. She picked up.

"The lady has a gun, and is firing at Marty. Trying to kill him."

One of the stable assistants grabbed the phone at the far end of the huge barn, and dialed Angela.

"Marty and the lady came back to the farm, and when the children were gone, she exploded. She accused Marty of sending them with Mary. First, she whacked him with a shovel. He got up, and moved away from her. After, she went to her car, and picked up a gun."

"Was he hit? Shot, I mean?"

"Not as far as I know. Nevertheless, a two-year-old filly was hit twice by bullets and killed."

Angela asked, "Have you called the police?"

"Not so far, I called you."

"Get everyone off the ranch. I'll call the authorities."

"Oh my God, she just fired off a barrage with her automatic."

Angela could hear a steady gunfire in the background, and corresponding screams. The phone went dead. Angela called the sheriff's department, and telephoned Duke. He answered on the second ring.

"Hey, honey. I'll be at the ranch in three minutes. Are you at the barn?" Duke asked.

"No. I'm off the farm. The bitch has gone ballistic with a gun. She's killed a horse. Maybe, Marty?"

"You're gone, right?"

"Yes."

"The children?"

"The kids are out on a ride. I am up at Mary's ranch. I told Sylvia to get everyone else off the ranch. Marty is at risk. He's at Cummings Valley Ranch – where I don't know."

"Okay. I have the picture. Have you called the sheriff?"

"Yes. Just called."

"I'll make an assessment. Probably, will wait for law enforcement. I'll keep you informed by cell phone."

Duke Snyder arrived at the ranch in his Chevrolet Bronco, which he kept in his hanger at the local airport. The trainer pulled off the side of the road at the front of the farm.

Cummings Valley Ranch had a picturesque entrance with a sign with the name of the farm spanning two brick pillars. Two-foot tall lights adorned the brick standards, as well. White plank fencing, which enclosed paddocks, attached to the pillars. Moreover, the farm had brilliant colored plants, which were changed to fit the season.

It was clear to any visitor these owners cared deeply for the facility and the animals on it.

There was a 40-foot wide road running down the center between three significant paddocks on each side of the entrance road. After the third paddock, the road separated, with the right fork taking you to the barn, the center road leading to Duke and Angela's home at the ranch, and the left fork heading to other smaller dwellings, including Marty's ranch home.

Duke got out of his Bronco holding a Megaphone. The normal usage was to communicate with riders on the farm's track. Today, he was going to use the device as a broadcast center to control the situation – hopefully, wrangle in Marty's wife without injury.

Ranch workers were climbing over fences – running through paddocks, finding freedom from the lunatic inside the barn.

"Everyone, come here to the entrance to the farm," Duke ordered. Workers were complying.

He raised the megaphone again, "Cheri put down your weapon. Law enforcement is on their way. Cheri this is lunacy. Do not hurt anyone. Don't hurt yourself." Duke pleading for calm.

Immediately, Duke's position came under fire. He was a half-mile away from Cheri. At that distance, her accuracy was limited. However, anyone could be hit by chance. She fired off a clip with two shells hitting his car.

The good thing about her shooting at him, it was taking the others out of the line of fire.

"I wonder how many clips she may have. Most people don't carry an arsenal with them. She must have anticipated something like this."

Silence – farm employees huddled behind Duke's vehicle. In the distance, sirens whaled.

Duke saw Cheri get in her vehicle. Clearly, she heard the sirens as well. Plain she was going to make a run for freedom. Duke ran over to the metal gate, which normally remained unlocked during the day – swung it closed. He padlocked the gate. He yelled at everybody to get in his car, or run further down the road – away from the gate.

There were too many people to fit in the vehicle; but under these circumstances, people found a seat quickly — on laps, and on the floor. The others scattered. Duke floored his Bronco.

Down at the end of the furthest paddock, Duke stopped. Everyone piled out of the car. Again, they hid behind it.

Shortly, two sheriff cars careened to the ranch. At the same time, Cheri screeched toward the now-closed farm gate. She was traveling at a high rate of speed. Seeing the gate closed, she braked.

Getting out of her car, Cheri took aim at the three officers who had piled out of their sheriff's vehicle. She was crazy — beyond reason. She lifted her gun and fired at the officers – she hit one of the deputies in the head. He immediately went down — dead before he reached the ground.

The other two officers took a position behind their squad car. They started returning fire — shooting to kill. Even so, it appeared, for the moment, that Cheri possessed better skill.

At this time, no one knew the present location of Marty Torres. He was the target of Cheri's anger. Perhaps, already dead – leaving the children orphaned.

Cheri's car was riddled with bullet holes; however, she eluded injury. This devil appeared invincible. The same could not be said for a second officer who had been felled by the lunatic.

"My goodness," winced Duke, "How did she learn to shoot?"

In the distance, more sirens announced they were heading to the farm. Only one major artery leads into Cummings Valley. Therefore, making an assault on the ranch takes time.

"Cheri, this is hopeless – very wrong," urged Duke by loudspeaker. Two shots rang out toward his location. Nevertheless, everyone there was well protected, cowering behind the car.

Duke, as a private investigator, had been severely injured while investigating on another remote ranch in Otay Mesa near San Diego. Not the type to back down. Nevertheless, he was unarmed.

Sensing her situation was becoming more hopeless, Cheri got back in her vehicle. Staying low in the seat, she backed her car some distance further away from the locked gate.

"She's retreating," said a worker.

"Hope so."

Unexpectedly, Cheri floored her vehicle and came straight at the gate, intending to ram her way through. She hit the gate going 50 miles an hour. The gate crumbled, giving way to the impact. A portion of the brick pillar plummeted to the ground. Cheri appeared in a manic state, and again eluded injury.

"Is she impervious to death," questioned Toni.

"Devils are momentarily — before righteousness wins out," Duke replied.

After the collision with the gate, Cheri continued on. She turned left out of the farm, passing the lone confused officer, who was scrunched down behind his car. Cheri plugged him twice as she fled.

"He was cowering — no reason to shoot him," said a groom.

Toni said, "Someone will make a movie about this. She's deadlier than Bonnie of Bonnie and Clyde."

Duke knew for certain. "Cheri was pure evil."

All the law enforcement initially summoned to the farm lay bleeding.

Duke said, "Incredible, she outgunned three trained officers."

"Only in our hamlet is that possible," said a groom.

"She's had professional training," said another groom.

Duke had the good sense to call the sheriff station. Otherwise, Cheri was going to run headlong into the additional sheriff cars racing to the ranch.

"Yes, this is Duke Snyder. I am the owner and operator of Cummings Valley Ranch. The assailant that opened fire on the ranch has now shot the three dispatched officers. She is fleeing out of Cummings Valley. She is armed and dangerous," said Duke to the dispatcher.

"We'll be waiting for her. Don't worry."

"I'm sure that's what the first group of keystone cops said," Duke replied.

This time the officers took defensive positions behind their cars, which were set as a barricade, blocking the both lanes.

Cheri ran headlong into the trap. Seeing the vehicles blocking the highway, she was in such a state she believed she could run through the cars, as she had buckled the gate.

"Fire," said the sergeant. Six-armed sheriff's deputies opened up on her vehicle as it barreled down on them. Three deputies had shotguns, one a rifle and two pistols.

"Damn," said the lunatic — pushing the pedal to the floor.

"Crazy," cried the sergeant.

Cheri's car traveled more than 100 miles per hour. The vehicle ran straight into a sheriff's van, stretching across to the roadway. The resulting crash upended the sheriff's car. Pushing it off the highway into a drainage ditch — officers and all. An immense plume of smoke rose in the air; the boom sounded ten miles away.

The sergeant, armed with a shotgun, fired dead blank into Cheri's now crushed car. There was no way prior to the officer's shotgun-barrage for Cheri to have escaped death. The explosion from the resulting crash would have barbequed the witch. Nonetheless, he was not taking any further risk.

"Eat in hell tonight," said the sergeant coldly.

After, the sergeant reported to dispatch. "Dead here — two of our men—crushed by her car, when it rammed us. Also, dead is the suspect who has a variety of injuries. Cause of her death will be sorted out by the coroner. I know I fired a shotgun point blank," reported the sergeant to headquarters.

**Back at Cummings Valley Ranch.**

Duke told the farm employees to walk slowly to the barn using the main road leading into the farm.

"I want to assess any risk to you. I'm driving — will stop momentarily at the front gate. I want to see what help we can provide the officers."

The trainer drove to the front of Cummings Valley Ranch. Approaching the squad car, Duke stooped beside one officer who was still alive. Two others were dead.

"911, what is your emergency?"

"This is Duke Snyder at Cummings Valley Ranch. We have an officer shot at this location. He needs immediate assistance. Two other officers are dead. We may have other injuries at our farm. Please send three emergency ambulances."

The operator asked, "Is this where the lady collided into the sheriff's vehicles?"

"No, this is at Cummings Valley Ranch. This is the first location. This is where she shot the injured officer as she extricated herself from our farm."

The lady said, "We need emergency vehicles for the other location as well, but we will dispatch at least one for the fallen officer. Advise if there are any other injuries at your location when you know."

Duke, further appraising the situation, said, "I will keep that in mind. However, the shooting started here. Be aware."

"Right."

When two other farm members reached the injured officer, Duke gave instructions on how best to help him until paramedics arrived.

"I'm going on the ranch to find Marty. Betty is still missing. Does anyone know where they are?

Everyone shook their heads.

Apprehensively, Duke retrieved his Bronco. He drove hastily into the farm.

"I guess her mental illness has been apparent — we all stayed as far away from her as we could," Duke thought. "I don't know if anyone even tried to help her. Sure, she was crazy. However, I take time to help an injured horse. Why not time for her?"

He was sober, and angry at the inaction. Remorseful. "Every person deserves our attention — crazy or not. The ill need our help – more."

No answer apparent, Duke drove quickly to the barn. The edifice is very extensive. It is impossible to know the immediate location of anyone, or to find someone quickly.

"I'm going to install barn speakers, tomorrow," Duke thought to himself. "Now that the horse is out of the barn — no laughing matter."

Duke said through his megaphone, "Marty and anyone else who is hiding on the farm, Cheri is gone. She drove away. If you are hiding, come out. Otherwise, I will look for you. Please, acknowledge."

The sound hardly made a dent in the gigantic structure.

He ran through the facility as quickly as he could — looking into each stall. The horses were agitated. They were pacing their stalls, and some of them were rearing.

"It's going to take weeks to get them back to normality," Duke reasoned. However, his first thoughts were on his missing comrades.

Duke came to a feed-room, where hay, straw, oats, and other materials are kept. He heard moaning.

"I'm here."

Duke saw the injured employee, with blood oozing from a leg. Duke took off one of the cords, which held the straw bale together, and wrapped it as a tourniquet around the leg. His actions stopped the blood flow.

Duke called 911.

"This is Snyder. We have a gunshot victim in our gigantic barn. Dispatch an ambulance. Injury is serious. The slug is to a main artery in the leg. I have applied a tourniquet. I am not a paramedic; therefore, my actions are temporary."

"Stay with the victim, loosen the tourniquet every five minutes, and then retighten. Use good judgment. Don't let her bleed out."

"I understand, but I have to search for another possible victim. I will return to this injured person within five minutes."

"What is your ETA to our barn here at Cummings Valley Ranch?"

"Unfortunately, we are stretched impossibly thin. It will be fifteen minutes."

"Okay, I'll keep you informed."

Duke looking sympathetic said, "I need to leave for just a minute or two. I need to find Marty Torres. Do you have any idea where he is?

"No," said the injured woman shakily. "Please don't leave me here alone."

"I won't for long. I do have to leave for a minute or two. I promise I'll be right back."

"No, please."

Duke sprinted away. He looked helplessly into stalls as he ran along. He was yelling, "Marty, Marty – yell out if you hear me."

Keeping an eye on his watch, Duke searched the immense barn as thoroughly as he could. He noted that four minutes had elapsed, since he had last been with the injured employee.

Returning to the feed room, Duke found the employees slumped nearly unconscious on the floor. Duke loosened the tourniquet. Blood spurted from the leg. Duke did not really know what he was doing, but treated the employee as if she was an injured horse.

"That's the best I can do. Next, I need to get you help – now."

Refastening the tourniquet, Duke picked up Betty as if she was a small filly. He trotted as quickly as he could to his vehicle. Headed toward the front gate.

When he got to the gate, he saw the injured officer had been whisked away.

"How long ago did the ambulance leave?"

"Maybe a minute."

Duke gave instructions to the employees.

"Marty is still missing. Run and find him. I have searched the barn end, which is closest to the main highway. Concentrate your search on the other half. Call me on the barn phone when you locate him. I'm taking Betty to an ambulance or the hospital. We can't lose her."

The employees were quick to action. All were fit from working with the horses — showed it by their athletic ability — climbing over fences, running through the paddocks toward the barn.

Duke was as quick, as well. He floored his Bronco, marching of toward town.

Duke reached the crash site where Cheri and two officers had lost their lives. No ambulances present. However, two sheriff's vehicles remained.

"I have a badly injured person in my backseat. She has been shot. I have applied a tourniquet. I have summoned an ambulance – have been told there are none."

Duke, the bottom-line-man, continued, "She needs to be taken to the hospital by you – now. One officer rides in the back, and administers assistance to Betty. The other drives with the siren wailing," Duke said, barking out orders. "Check with the paramedics. I don't really know what to do for the injury during travel."

The deputies responded immediately. Duke placed Betty in the back of the patrol car. The vehicle raced to the hospital.

Just as rapidly, Duke returned to Cummings Valley Ranch. The search was still underway when Duke returned to the barn. No one found Marty Torres, a groom told the trainer.

Duke said, "I'm going to see if Marty made it back to his house. You guys keep searching. Call me."

The trainer again raced in his quest to find his friend. No one present Marty's home. Duke retraced his steps to the central ranch road; turned and went toward the beautiful farmhouse.

After parking in the circular driveway, he sprinted up to the front door. Entering the home, he called for Marty.

"No answer."

Duke ran through the living room and into the kitchen. No Marty.

He ran into the service porch, and found blood everywhere. The smallish room had a washer and dryer, and freezer along one wall. The back door, leading from the yard, was open.

Barely inside the back door, two bloody handprints streaked the washing machine, with blood flowing downward to the floor.

There on the floor lay Marty.

Duke could not immediately grasp whether his brother-in-law was alive or dead. From appearances, no person could survive the blood loss.

Without a moment's pause, Duke dialed 911.

"911 operator."

"This is Duke Snyder, again. Send an ambulance to my home at Cummings Valley Ranch immediately. My farm manager Marty Torres has been shot. He is bleeding profusely."

"Mr. Snyder, we are out of ambulances or medical response vehicles."

"What in the hell..." Duke said.

A different voice – broke into the line.

"This is rescue helicopter, Rescue 1."

"Where are you?" Duke asked urgently.

"Cummins."

"You mean Cummings Valley?"

"Yep."

"Land at the big house – not the barn. Repeating... helicopter land at the main – the large house – the primary ranch home." The normally unflappable Duke Snyder could hardly speak.

"I understand."

Duke knelt to feel the pulse of his friend Marty Torres. He was surprised. Marty had a weak and thready pulse.

"But he has one." Duke was already kneeling by his friend – looked upward. "Heavenly father, please be with us."

The trainer considered rolling Marty over; but believed his position on his stomach compressing his wounds might be saving his life.

"Leave well enough alone."

Only a minute later, Duke heard the whoosh of the blades from the helicopter setting down in the front yard.

Duke ran out the back door, and around the side of the house toward the helicopter. Distinct blood droplets stained the grass and driveway. Evident Marty Torres was leading the shooter away from the barn – if possible.

"Where is the victim?"

"Over here."

No wasted words or motion. These were professionals. The best.

Paramedics from the hospital trauma unit quickly assessed the farm manager's plight. Shot five times. However, God miraculously was on Marty's side that day. Not one bullet hit a vital organ. Yes, there was a lot of blood.

"God and Jesus had compassion. It might not always appear so," Duke thought. "Nonetheless, if we as humans stop our moaning for a second, we can feel the Lord's grace. Mercy for two kids already cheated out of their childhood."

Marty was critical. Spared death, because of quick action of the trauma paramedics. Had the manager been loaded into an ambulance he would have died without the proficient assistance he received.

Within three minutes, the paramedics had Marty loaded aboard the well-equipped flying bird, which was winging its way toward a Bakersfield hospital. This trip would be much quicker than over bumpy roads.

"It's obvious Marty's intent had been to pull the gunfire away from the barn. He was willing to give up his life by getting out. He hoped he could draw Cheri away," Duke thought.

Again, Duke lamented the travesty. Could it have been avoided by forcing Cheri to get mental help?

"What right did I have? Even so, to do nothing."

He knew California had long ago closed its hospitals for the mentally ill. In recent years, due to budget constraints, they no longer even afforded long-term assistance at local hospitals or clinics.

If a mentally ill patient refused treatment, many were left to the streets. Cheri was doggedly strong. She would terrorize anyone into giving into her demands.

Law enforcement many times made an error in believing female combatants were innocent, when deciding between their male counterparts.

"If Marty had defended himself, his butt would have been toast."

Cheri used this to her advantage repeatedly. She was an attractive lady, who could entice men.

"She would do anything. A black widow."

Once she was in their bed, Cheri would take advantage until she had cleaned out her victim. When one was broke, she would move on to another. She was the perpetual snake, a venomous one. All of her victims were glad to see her gone.

"They would pay her to leave."

All ended up knowing she was ill. However, no one took the risk of helping her. All were glad to say, "Good riddance."

# Chapter 18

**Decision Time in the Valley.** The early evening started to settle on the high plains, with dew and haze bringing a chill. The children returned from their ride – Tehachapi and Nina strolling back to the small colt's stall.

"I already feel something is wrong," said the young, but mature child, who had aged too quickly because of hardship; nevertheless, would have another mountain piled on tonight.

Tehachapi himself is no normal two-year-old. His existence at Cummings Valley Ranch bleak in the early going. Only Nina saved him from standing in a dusty field in some far-off place. Or, sold to a killer outfit that made dog food.

"Yes. Something ominous is present; I agree."

The colt had not experienced death. Nonetheless, the events hung strong in the air. Sometimes parents believe young children do not sense loss; nonetheless, they are closer to God – from whence we all came.

"What matters—you!" I told her.

"No, you too."

Angela acted with wisdom in bringing Tehachapi to the ranch. No matter how great a horse racing he might become, the diminutive colt is effective medicine for Nina.

Angela alerted by Duke to return to the farm—the danger now eradicated. He did not inform his wife on the phone of the total disaster—not all. Only what was needed to bring her to him.

"Just come home, honey," he had urged.

"The kids?"

"They're fine. Home—please."

She understood by the tenor of his voice that all was not well. By the time Nina and her brother started riding toward the big barn; Duke was out in front flagging them.

"Come here," he urged.

In the clear air, Duke's voice bounced off the mountains. Reverberating. Duke, normally, was quiet around the children, because he had not been around many. These two—he loved with all his heart. Even so, he was not quite sure what to say. He needed Angela. He had to tread water with the children until his wife appeared.

"Calm down," he cautioned himself.

The children put away their horses at the urging of their uncle. Nina, on most days, would stay out until hunger drove her to the dinner table, but she was exhausted. The emotion—draining energy.

Angela arrived home minutes afterward with Duke taking his wife into his arms. He held her, transmitting his love more soothingly than words.

Nina limped into the kitchen where Duke and Angela hugged. Tommy followed.

"Children, come and sit down." Duke said, leading them out of the massive kitchen.

He ushered them into the living room and sat them next to their aunt on the long sofa. The room decorated by Angela for formal events at the ranch, but still showed her heart and warmth. A large front window peered out at the paddocks and the picturesque horse nursery.

They sat on the eleven-foot couch, which rested under a five foot by eight-foot painting by Hudson River School painter Thomas Cole. The scene itself was somber. The brown and yellow tones used by the master artist were inspirational.

"Listen," said Duke – not a man to preface his comments. Everyone knew his nature. Understood they would get the bottom line—whatever, he was going to tell them.

"Your mother is dead."

There it was. No sugar coating. Nonetheless, the children could tell by the softness in Duke's voice that he loved them.

"She was involved in a fatal accident today while going to town," he reported. Duke intentionally left out the details, including her involvement at the ranch.

For the children, there was relief and anguish. Their mother had abused them—yet, she was still there mom. Hence, their feelings were mixed.

Duke added, "Additionally, your dad is in the hospital. He was injured as well."

Tommy, who was much closer to his father than Nina, asked, "Is dad going to be okay?"

He was crying. Trying to hold the tears in check, but he could not.

"He left here by helicopter about an hour ago. He is in surgery in Bakersfield. We will not know anything for several more hours."

This was news to Angela, as well.

"Shouldn't we be going to the hospital?" Angela said.

Duke had time to reflect more than his wife did. He sought calm. Wanted to protect the children and his wife from heartache.

"I think we are all hungry and exhausted. The ride to the hospital will take time. When we get there, no one will be able to tell us anything. I suggest we eat, clean up a little, and let me check things out."

It was clear the three onlookers wanted to sprint off down the mountain to Bakersfield.

"Let me see if I can get a helicopter to pick us up. Check and see how much longer they expect the surgery to take. It's possible they will fly Marty to Los Angeles or San Francisco. He was badly injured."

Duke was stalling. He did not want the children, or for that matter, his wife at the hospital if Marty died. For the children, their entire support system would be wiped out in one afternoon. Mom and father.

"Angela, one of the farm workers has volunteered to bring in food. She will be here in about thirty minutes. Let the children take a quick shower. I'll call the hospital, and we can report everything we know."

Reluctantly, she agreed.

Tommy and Nina were sent upstairs to take a warm shower. Both children had been outside all day. It was clear to Duke; they were cold and hungry. They were filthy from their afternoon jaunting on horseback. Nina's face streaked with dirt and sweat.

With the children upstairs, Duke again took Angela in his arms. Then, sat her on the couch.

"I've been thinking since Marty left in the chopper. I think he may die. The children will be without any parent. Even if he lives, it's going to take considerable time for him to rehabilitate."

"What?" said Angela, not fully understanding.

She got it that Marty was severely injured.  She understood he might die.  She also appreciated Duke reasoning to keep the children away from the hospital in the interim.

There was something more.  Something between the lines that her lover did not yet communicate. What was it?

Duke looked her squarely in the eyes. "I know you've questioned my expansion of our training barns throughout the country. Potentially, reckless."

Angela's eyes bored into her husband intently. She saw a softness in Duke's demeanor.

"Until this afternoon, I really did not understand. Now, I get it. Family is first.  The kids upstairs are our family.  You…and those kids…are the foundations. They are the bedrock we must protect.  I realize—now.  I understand what you have been patiently telling me these months.

He went on. "I believe we must consolidate immediately.  We should keep our race barns in Southern California and here on the ranch.  We have expert staff at both track facilities."

Angela agreed with her husband's statements, nodding her head in enthusiastic affirmation.  Tears were forming in her eyes — her heart whaling up with love for this man.

"I believe you must stay full-time on the ranch with the children until  Marty is well.  You will have to be mother to those two."

Tears of love flowed from Angela's eyes.  She loved Duke almost from first sight.  His tender relationship with his horses told of the character of the man.

"If Marty lives, we must give Marty and Mary time to sort out their relationship. They appear to have the makings of a family. If they indeed marry, we must help them assimilate the children into their lives," Duke said.

Angela could not speak. She choked with emotion.

"I'm going to try to get the best horses from the eastern owners to come west. In any case, I am going to sell my barns in the East as soon as possible. Some of my assistant trainers are ready to go out on their own – I will help them finance if they want."

The formation of the **Cummings Valley Pact** did not take two minutes. However, heartfelt plan would be the foundation of their lives and of the children for decades.

"I believe we can break, train, and ultimately race our own horses directly from the farm. Obviously, they will have to qualify with works at the track. Even so, horses such as Tehachapi can start the tradition."

"It's hard to think Tehachapi can be the foundation of anything except the love of a little girl. Holding her together." Angela said.

"You guys thought he was too small and too slow," said Duke. "I believe he is his father, No Rain, revisited. Horses win with heart. That little girl injected his heart with get-up-and-go."

He was now smiling.

Angela took Duke's face with both hands and pulled him to her. She kissed him like a teenager. She pulled him as close to her as physically possible. Their mouths and bodies merged as one.

She said, "What is important to me, in addition to saving these children, is having a child of our own. I want you around enough to be certain that a little Duke is in me soon."

There could be no question that Duke Snyder had built a racing dynasty. It could have lasted forty or fifty years. No other trainer in America had such dominance.

His loving training style created a new direction in American horse racing.

No one claimed that Duke was the best administrator. However, no one denied his relationship with the horse was next to none. Duke— sweepingly— decided family comes first.

Before fame. Before raising young horses into champions. He decided he wanted to help his own child become a person of value and love God.

# Chapter 19

**Marty Torres lived.** Angela and Duke did not embark on the trip to the hospital that evening. News had reached them the operation had been successful. Nevertheless, doctors reported Marty would not be permitted visitors until the next day.

"He's doing better," Mary told to Nina from the Bakersfield surgery center.

To Nina, Mary said, "Your dad says you have to watch over Cummings Valley Ranch and the warmblood until he can get back on his feet. Talk it over with Tehachapi. He says you don't make decisions alone."

### True to his word.

Duke is a master on the telephone, employing a warm, loving instinct. He burned up the lines to the East. Within days, he located suitable replacements for his racing operations, winding down his involvement. Some he sold – others he closed.

He was able to maintain a major Kentucky multi-millionaire and his farm as race clients. The owner's horses moved west to The Great Race Place – Santa Anita.

### Meeting at Tehachapi.

Duke called the Cummings Valley Summit — his four best leaders brought to the farm.

"You four are going to be largely responsible for our horses at Hollywood Park and Santa Anita. We've had enough time together now, with split barns, that this new concept presents no inherent difficulties. In fact, I think the plan allows us to focus," said Duke to the trusted four.

Scrap said, "I believe this new direction is far better. I know Angela does."

"Yes," she agreed.

Duke said, "We are going to start anew. We are going to improve the track at the ranch. Horses which are owned by Angela and me will be housed here, and be trucked to Hollywood or Santa Anita to run."

Angela asked, "You going to employee more of the European method of training. Galloping horses a greater distance over open ground?"

"Yes. At least, I am going to try to utilize that concept with No Rain offspring. They obviously want to run longer. Nina has already proven the notion with Tehachapi."

Duke's mind wandered to the summer spent long ago in England. There, he toiled for four months for a top-flight English trainer. He remembered the morning gallops over the hillside behind the trainer's yard.

In England, instead of having stalls at a racetrack, trainers have their own yards near or joining their home.

Duke's training-friends exchanged ideas in a daylong meeting that went well into the night. Ultimately, everyone agreed the change might prove wildly successful.

"It will take some work," Duke said.

Little did everyone know how true those words were? There was no one at the ranch who was not touched by the decisions.

Nina and Tommy joined the group in early evening. The conversations went on during dinner. The food was not exciting because a farmhand had brought it in from a local café in town.

"I think we need to get a cook," said Nina seriously. "Angela works harder than anyone. Dad's in the hospital. More people will be working at the farm if you guys are going to train here. Instead of having the workers leave for an hour or two at lunch, there should be some sort of cafeteria."

Everyone looked at Nina in astonishment. She was always practical and bottom line. Her body might be broken, but her brain was not.

Duke winked at Nina, "You're right. We need someone doing the cooking. Need a cafeteria, more stall space, a better track, and probably some good living quarters making a desirable place for the best grooms."

"Right now, the big barn will handle thirty horses in training," said Angela. "That's with taking all the pipe corrals and temporary stalls out. The arena can be enlarged, so I can break horses 365 days a year—out of the weather."

Scrap asked, "Duke, how many horses in training do you see here at any given time?"

"I don't know."

"You don't want to build a million stalls until you are certain the plan will work. Furthermore, you can't have your stallion, No Rain, around the other horses – especially mares. You probably need to have a mare barn, unless you are going to keep them in the fields or in pipe corrals."

"Certainly, there is a lot to think about," Duke agreed.

Angela said, "No Rain is a gentleman. Even as the breeding stallion, he has a good sense. We can give him one of the larger stalls near the vet room."

Nina said, "Turn him out in a pasture during the day."

"Agreed."

"If we keep two foaling stalls, there should be enough in the interim. A foaling stall will take up the space of two regular horse boxes."

Duke was following his bride's suggestion.

"We will have twenty four regulation stalls for training horses. The question revolves around how many two-year-olds and the young horses will take up the stalls, while they're being broken and trained for the races."

"Right."

Duke said, "We can all see more stalls are required, if our concept of racing and training off Cummings Valley ranch is going to work."

Angela nodded. "Sure. We've got to make the ranch so you don't have the burden of flying from the track to the farm every day."

"The flight is less than half an hour."

Angela bristled, gently, "You've got to drive to the airport, to and from, plus the flight. That is more than an hour getting to Hollywood Park. When they are racing at Santa Anita or Del Mar the time is tripled."

Silence filled the dining room. Was not the great food that had everybody's tongue. It was clear Duke's decision was gargantuan. His love for Angela and his duty for the children lingered.

"Flying is therapy for me," Duke countered.

Angela knew this to be true. Nevertheless!

"I also know flying when you are exhausted into bad weather kills."

"I still have the apartment in Marina del Rey. If the weather is bad, I will stay there."

"We are back to being separated. That is the purpose of training at the ranch – so we can tell bedtime stories to each other. Right?

Tommy said quizzically, "You guys tell bedtime stories?"

Angela looked tenderly at Duke saying, "As many nights as we can. That's how families have babies."

These children were raised at a breeding farm. They were not the multitude of the young, who had no concept of birth.

"Aunt Angela, we've seen horses breeding. Dad has been honest in explaining life," said Nina. "I've watched hundreds of babies being born on the farm. I helped with Tehachapi when he was born. Everybody was watching the Derby – so I helped."

"You're right. I cannot fool you two. With men and women, husbands and wives, there is love and commitment exchanged. We make 'love'—then babies are made," she said tenderly.

"Unlike stallions who breed many mares, a husband makes love with only his wife," Angela explained.

She wanted the children to understand the difference between what took place between stallions and mares in the breeding shed, and what took place between men and women.

"I know you guys love each other," Nina said, touching her aunt's hand.

"How can you tell?" Duke asked.

Nina replied, "Easy. You cannot keep your hands off her. She can't keep her eyes off of you."

Tommy added, "The reason you're going to race off the ranch is because you guys want to be together. I guess you want to see us too?

"Absolutely. And it's because Angela and I love you and your sister."

Nina asked, "Where will Tommy and I live?"

Nina again with the bottom line.

"Honey, we are going to work that out – don't you worry. You will stay with us until your dad is comes home. Once he is back at the farm, we'll see how fast he can take care of both of you."

"What about Mary?" Nina asked with concern. Her love apparent. How old was this child? Angela peered at her in amazement. Nina was trying to figure out relationships.

"How do you feel about Mary?" Angela asked.

"I think dad loves her. He was very lonely before they met. He's different now – alive."

Angela did not let Nina off the hook.

"Sweetie, I didn't ask how your dad felt; I was wondering about you."

Nina was perceptive for her young age. She looked around the table. Peered at people she did not know very well.

"I like her. She's nice to me. Mom is dead. Mother always hurt Tommy and me; didn't love us."

Tears filled her eyes.

Angela thought, "These children needed to feel God's love. Need to understand 'love' includes them. Feel tenderness and compassion."

Duke saw the anguish, as well.

"The farm could save these two children. Nina, more than Tommy, is crippled by a loveless life. Her leg is the least of her misery," he whispered to Angela.

"This man got it," sensed Angela. "His heart is part of what makes me love him so much."

Duke had always been a horse whisperer. Knowledgeable people at the track often said, "Duke, talks to horses." Duke's relationship with the animals was uncanny. Sometimes with people, he was "a little slow," according to Nina.

"He would always come around, but slow to get us," she had told Angela.

No one suggested Duke had supernatural ability. Clearly incredible – sometimes even weird, bizarre and mysterious how the trainer instinctively "just knew" things' horses were feeling.

Not people.

It was indeed eerie and creepy when Duke found an undiagnosed ailment or miraculously made a change in training that led to an unearthly improvement.

Even with being "slow" to understand people—especially young children, the uncle understood Nina. Better than most. They were very alike—in one way. Duke felt he understood Nina's affinity to Tehachapi, for example. He got the vibe when Nina said she actually talked to the colt.

"There was no doubt Nina and the colt understood each other perfectly."

Whether she could actually speak to Tehachapi, Duke doubted. He believed her closeness was born of separation – especially for a mother. And for a father who worked too hard — almost to abandonment.

"Give her time. In fact, God gives us time," Duke said, putting his hand on Angela's knee. In the meantime, we have each other – and Nina has Tehachapi."

The little girl said, questioning, "Yes. I love him. You are not taking him away from me, are you?"

"No."

"Oh, I was so afraid I was going to lose him too."

Nina knew of claiming races at racetracks—where owners could simply buy a horse right out of a race. Duke and Angela would retire the little tyke before putting him at risk.

"You tell Tehachapi he is one of the major reasons we are going to race off of the farm," Duke said, his voice cracking.

Nina got up from her chair. She went around the table and put her arms around Duke, giving him a giant hug. She stood on her tiptoes trying to give him a kiss, which landed somewhere below his ear on his neck. She was not quite tall enough to reach his cheek.

She did reach his heart.

# Chapter 20

**Hoof Bruises and Mystery at Cummings Valley.** With 24 horses in training, others being broken, and still more foals walking on lead ropes. The goings-on at Cummings Valley ranch exciting. Busy.

Almost, too much for the small number of the farm hands.

Additionally, there was additional excitement when Marty came home. His injuries had been life threatening. Doctors – largely because of pressure from insurance companies who pay the medical bills – chase people from the hospital bed before they are entirely healed. Nina's dad was no exception.

Marty would need several months of therapy before he could resume his duties on the ranch. Even, getting around his small house required assistance.

Mary and Marty had to work out their feelings. Marty understood why he had been chased from Mary's bedroom; however, he was hurt deeply by that demand, as well.

He realized, better now, the reason for getting married before playing house. He found himself on the street when the first thing went wrong. Marty was critical in a number of ways—more than just from bullet wounds. His heart wounded deeply.

Angela told Duke, "Marty had nearly as much heartache as Nina with the crazy lady. It came close to killing him. He has pulled inside himself—shut everyone out." Cheri had always played Marty with unrealistic and cruel demands.

Therefore, when Mary told him, he could not share her bed, as long as Cheri was with him at the ranch, it was as if a knife sliced into the heart. Cheri might be in his bed. However, Marty was not sleeping with her. In any sense, other than they were in the same bed when they fell asleep. Cheri wanting to cause bedlam.

Mary was in Marty's heart. Always.

Mary had relationship difficulties with other men, which caused her to distrust. Men had cheated on her – left her in a ditch. Marty felt he did not deserve the ire. He was not cheating.

The differences between men and women a struggle without open communications and trust are, as they say, deeper than the deep-blue sea.

Marty returned to his home at the ranch. As much as Mary felt betrayed, Marty suffered the same lonesome misery.

"Come on home with me," Mary urged.

"No. I think the children have been through enough. I want to be with you. Nonetheless, until we have worked out some things I believe it is best not to confuse them further."

Marty fooled no one. The children were not confused. He was. His pride was tender. Raw.

"Okay," she said. "But you watch; those kids aren't giving up their rooms at Angela's until things are settled here with us. Your stubbornness will leave you alone."

Of course, she was right.

Marty's ranch home was tiny. You entered into a tinny living room and dining room, which were about twelve-by-twelve, and an extremely little kitchen – four-by-six feet. Two people could not fit in the kitchen at the same time. There were two small bedrooms with a bathroom between. The whole house was about seven hundred square feet.

"I'll be fine here. Duke hired a cook who can give me food."

Mary said, "Suit yourself."

The children put down roots with Duke and Angela. There was a certainty—they were not moving.

"Love my dad, but Angela understands me," Nina told Tommy. The little boy was not quite so certain. He always was drawn to Marty.

"Well, while they are figuring out things, I have chores to get done. Racing here will be difficult."

So, the children stayed put in the large home with Duke and Angela. As Mary predicted, Marty was very much alone.

Duke was always quick to action, and spent time improving the track Marty Torres built.

"If we're racin' off the ranch, the track has to be pristine," Duke told the family.

"Pristine? What's that?" asked Nina. "Something you feed horses?"

Everyone laughed.

"Obtaining advice from a track consultant was a good idea," said the trainer. He hauled countless truckloads of material into Cummings Valley.

"You're so filthy," chided Angela, "You look as if you are in the trucking business."

"You never know," Duke answered wearily. "Could end up that way if we aren't careful.

Duke did not expand farm's track to a mile yet. He concentrated on improving the quality of the half-mile jaunt. A week after Duke had completed his modification; Nina took Tehachapi on a morning gallop on the track.

She returned to the barn with a grimace on her face.

"Tehachapi says his front right foot hurts," said Nina.

Tehachapi had been galloping in hopes of returning for a stake's race. However, he began to limp.

"Bring him over here," said Duke.

After piloting him to the trainer, Nina jumped down. Indeed, Tehachapi's right foot front was bruised.

"Pick up your left foot boy," said Duke. The colt without urging picked up his correct foot – standing on the right injured foot. It was unusual for any horse to rest on a lame leg. Duke was amazed.

"This one is bruised, as well."

"The back too," said Nina, inspecting.

Normally, Nina groomed Tehachapi. However, Duke summoned the most-experienced groom named Poncho to help.

"I have him scheduled to run in about three weeks. We can't afford to lose races if he's going to run in the Kentucky Derby," Duke lamented.

Poncho, looking at the feet, said, "They are bruised badly. The right one is the worst. We should get it x-rayed."

Four more horses came back lame from the morning workout. The works the morning before had gone without a hitch.

"Shut it down, Angela," Duke instructed.

Duke looked as if he was ready to cry. He had worked so tirelessly on the track — he could not believe he was maiming horses.

"What do you think it is? She asked.

"Don't know. I inspected every inch of the track last night. I watered it and tilled it this morning. It was perfect," said Duke.

Poncho agreed, "I had nothing to do last night, so I walked it as well. I have been concerned about working horses here at the farm."

Duke mounted his ranch pony horse Momentum, and Nina joined him on Tough Stuff. They were going to inspect.

"Tough Stuff is now your pony horse, huh," said Duke. "He was my constant companion before he was retired, you know?"

Nina's loving touches restored the aged horse to health.

"He's my second favorite," Nina replied.

Duke did not need to ask who her favorite was.

The duo tracked their animals on opposite sides of the fifty-foot wide remote racetrack. They took it slow, so they could inspect the riding surface.

"We may have to walk it," Duke conjectured. "Maybe, the offending element is somewhat below the surface."

The horses came out of the giant green barn and walked about one hundred feet before they walked directly onto the Cummings Valley ranch track. The animals had to walk by the starting gate in order to gain entrance.

Once on the track there was a straightaway. Nina and Duke were three-quarters of the way down the straightaway when Nina hollered.

"Uncle, over here."

"What did you find?"

"Jagged rocks."

"What?"

"Rocks."

Duke could not take Momentum directly across the track from his position, because of an outer rail, which protected the horses from running off. The trainer stopped and tied Momentum to the rail. Duke ducked under the rail walking toward Nina.

"Here too," he cried.

He said to himself, "This isn't my mistake. This is butchery."

Duke inspected the inner portion and discovered a three-foot section where sharp stones resided. The trainer tied ribbon to the rail, marking the portion.

"Angela, we found stones here," Duke said by phone. "Get some hands and walk entirety of the track. Nina and I will continue riding around it. After our lap, we will join you." Duke said.

Nina continued riding Tough Stuff around the oval. Most kids had the attention span of a gnat. Most children her age spent hours on the computer, playing games. Not her.

"Uncle Duke, there is another spot here too."

Nina meandered another eighty feet down the track.

"There are more stones here than where you are."

Duke remounted Momentum. He galloped down the outer rail and leapt off. It was clear this was no accident. It was impossible that two sections of the track had stones.

"Criminal," said Duke. "No accident."

Angela and three others marched around the half-mile track with rakes, intently surveying the expanse of the training surface.

After Nina and Duke were finished going around the oval, they rode to meet Angela.

"Nina, take Momentum back to the barn. Help Poncho with Tehachapi," Duke instructed.

Once Angela came to the rock outcropping, she too was inconsolable.

"Who could have done this?"

"Whoever put the rocks here was trying to ruin one of the animals," said Tom Fryer, a 65-year-old retired groom, who had come to the farm as an inexpensive place to live. He now helped with part-time duties.

"This was certainly intentional."

Duke agreed. "Take pictures. Dig the rocks out carefully. Keep them in the garage at the house. We are going to get, whoever did this."

Fryer said, "If I can use one of the motorized carts and a tractor, I'll take on this task. The track — you know."

"Good. You restore the track in two places. I'll have one of the kids walk around the rest checking to see if there are any other spots," Duke instructed.

Actually, Duke and Angela walked every inch. The only spots were the ones uncovered by Nina.

Duke was a detective, as well as a trainer. He solved more than a dozen cases for criminal attorney Cory Bentley. He was not stranger to intrigue.

"This is a mystery to me," he said.

"Normally, it's money, greed or sex that is the motive behind a criminal enterprise?" asked Angela.

"Yes, normally."

"This just doesn't make any sense," Angela responded. "Who would gain by hurting these horses? Was Tehachapi the target?" Angela questioned.

Duke thought for a moment.

"How could they even know that I was going to extend Tehachapi's gallops this morning? I just decided that in the middle of the night. It would be more likely that Nina would take him on a three-mile gallop through the valley. So, I don't believe Tehachapi himself was a target."

"Are we the target?"

"That would be fair to assume."

Duke and Angela returned to the barn. Angela was instructed to take the remaining horses on slow gallops through the valley and keep them off the track.

"We'll have to be careful where we train them, because if we follow too much of a routine someone will booby-trap that as well," Angela theorized.

"Right."

Duke meandered over to Tehachapi's stall and found Nina directly under Tehachapi's belly--where Scrap normally rested when he rubbed on horses.

"Bad idea," he said. "Even the calmest of horse can get spooked and step on you. I know Scrap sits there. At nearly 400 pounds, a horse would be afraid to step on him."

Nina responded, "Okay. When I groom other horses, I do it much more cautionary. With Tehachapi, we're like brother and sister."

"I'm sure in his time; Tommy has unintentionally hurt you, right."

"Yep."

"Tehachapi's many times larger than Tommy. He would squish you," Duke laughed.

Nina moved off to the right side of Tehachapi. She lifted his right foot and dug out mud, which had been applied by Poncho.

"What are you doing?" Duke asked in wonderment.

"Tehachapi's telling me to get the bruise portion of his foot dugout. That's what I'm attempting."

The trainer entered the stall, kneeling beside his niece. He was intent on instructing her that Poncho had years of experience dealing with injured animals. Before he could speak, Nina was prying with the hoof pick.

"Right here," said Tehachapi to Nina.

"Where?"

"A little lower down from where the pick is now," said Tehachapi.

Duke felt a strange sensation in the stall, but could not fully understand what was going on. He heard Tehachapi's pleas, but did not understand the language.

Nina lowered the position of the hoof pick.

"Right there," insisted Tehachapi.

Nina brought the leg to her eyes, so she could examine it closely. What she saw was a white splinter of a rock.

"Right here, uncle," Nina said to Duke.

Duke examined the hoof closely, seeing nothing other than the obvious bruises. He had not lifted Tehachapi's leg as near as Nina. Didn't raise hoof up to his eyes.

Nina sprinted off for a moment and returned with a fine pair of needle-nose pliers.

"What are you going to do with those?" Duke asked with concern.

"Watch."

By this time, Nina and Tehachapi drew a crowd. A number of workers came over to see what was going on.

Nina intuitively placed the tips of the pliers where she had been looking. However, she could not grasp the sliver.

"It hurts, get it out," complained Tehachapi.

"I will. Chill out," Nina instructed.

"Let me put a nail up your foot and see how you much you chill out," Tehachapi screeched.

Again, Duke could feel and hear tension, which he could not fully explain. He understood Tehachapi was in pain. He, however, could not translate the sounds into speech. As much as Duke understood the four-legged animals, it was clear Nina had Tehachapi's number.

Nina took the hoof pick and made a groove on each side of the splinter, which she detected in Tehachapi's foot.

Duke said, "Careful honey you'll lame him up for good if you are not exact. Let's get a vet."

Nina heard Duke's instructions; Nina heard Tehachapi more. She again picked up the needle-nose pliers. She put them over the sliver, which had now been exposed by her actions.

"Pull it quickly," Tehachapi urged.

Without a word, Angela held firmly and yanked back with her little hands. Even though miniature in size, Nina's hands gained strength riding a thousand miles through the valley on horses. They were vice strong.

When Nina pulled, Tehachapi screamed. Duke understood that language.

"Easy boy."

"Ouch," that hurt yelped Tehachapi.

"Got it," said Nina.

Tehachapi put his foot down. "That feels so much better."

Anxious to see if Nina had permanently lamed Tehachapi, Duke took the colt out of the stall on a lead rope.

He told Nina to walk Tehachapi, so he could examine how lame he was. Nina took the lead rope – unclipping it from his bridle.

"Tehachapi, walk down by the feed room and back," she instructed.

To everyone's astonishment, the colt did as instructed. It was not so much that he walked away without help, but that he stopped correctly at the feed room's door and turned. He walked back to Nina.

Duke was surprised for another reason. Tehachapi was no longer lame – not at all.

"Lamed him, huh?" said Nina, her eyes twinkling with delight.

# Chapter 21

**News Release—a Condemnation.**    Tehachapi was x-rayed. Poked and prodded.

"He walks sound, but all four feet are bruised," the veterinarian told Duke and Nina.

"One spot is deep--on the right foot, but all four are bruised. Thank goodness, there are no cracks. All will heal with time."

The vet gave Duke an ointment, with instruction to place the awful smelling stuff in all of Tehachapi's feet.

"Put it on for three days, clean each foot thoroughly.  Smear an extensive amount of the ointment on each foot, and have the shoer follow with pad.  Rest him this week, and after the short layoff, we will start to pony the brat.  As he is, he will be fine.  Keep an eye on him.  If he gets sore, stop," instructed the veterinarian.

Duke asked, "When do we pull the pads and check on his feet?"

"Two weeks."

Tehachapi said to Nina, "Let's see how this medicine works. Perhaps, we won't have to lose two weeks."

Nina nodded at her friend.  Again, Duke could tell communication was going on, but had no idea.

The next morning The Daily Racing Form printed an article from an undisclosed source, revealing Duke's plan to race from Cummings Valley ranch.  The article was particularly damaging because it said members of the Snyder staff were concerned.

"Vitally concerned."

"An injury to Duke Snyder's Tehachapi has already occurred at the farm during a routine galloping exercise," the Form reported. "The extent of the injury is not known. The informer told the racing form Tehachapi stepped on rocks, which were carelessly left on the training surface."

Duke was called for comment by the Form. Asked whether it was true, he planned to condition horses on an unapproved track in the mountains and ship horses to run at Santa Anita and Hollywood Park.

"What you're asking is partially true," he told The Daily Racing Form. "Every rule of the CHRB will be meticulously followed. Every horse running will have the required number of official works at the track, including gaining approval, before it starts," he said.

"While true that we plan to condition our two-year-olds at the farm, and some of my own horses, our barn will continue stabling client's horses at Hollywood Park and Santa Anita."

When asked about the injury to Tehachapi, Duke replied, "He sustained bruises to the bottom of his feet. The bruising is minor. Similar injuries occur at the track. As you know, my barn annually reports fewer layoffs from shin splints than any other stable. I do what is appropriate for the safety of the animals."

It was an hour after the Form had called that the chief steward from the track was on the line.

"Duke, we are concerned if any radical change is taking place in your training of horses."

"I have a long-standing record of excellence. I do not give restricted or banned medications to win races. I'm not changing anything that will affect the health of any horse," said Duke forcefully.

"It is true that I'm going to train some of my own horses here at the farm. Every one of them will meet the standards prescribed by the stewards. Every one of them will be available for inspection when they enter the track, inner a receiving barn or after a race."

The steward commented, "Duke, I have a lot of respect for you. Others have tried racing horses off farms. It just does not work. None of them have been successful." Warning, the steward continued, "I know you're not trying to skirt the rules. The tragedy is that your win percentage will suffer. You will lose owners and respect.

The trainer said, thoughtfully, in a respectful voice, "The minute I see any animal permanently damaged, I will stop. I hope my owners will give me the opportunity to experiment with my own horses. I'll train their horses, as I always have, from the track until I have proven that my new course works."

"Sounds reasonable."

"You are welcome to come to the farm. I'm training here as I learned in Europe."

When Duke got off the telephone, he had clear evidence someone was planning an assault on his reputation and his barn.

In the afternoon, Tom Fryers reported the two rock locations on the Cummings Valley track were repaired.

"I have walked every inch of the track, and it's ready to go."

Duke and Momentum galloped slowly around the track eyeing it for possible killing spots. Duke was not about to trust Fryers, even if the man had been the self-appointed track foreman.

"Tom is correct. The track has been repaired, and it's ready to resume training," Duke told Angela. "I'm going to gallop on it with a pony horse every morning I'm here. I'd appreciate it if you followed my lead when I'm at Hollywood Park. I don't think we can afford to trust anyone. Not right now."

Angela agreed. "Someone's up to mischief."

Nina reported that Tehachapi's feet were significantly better. "The veterinarian's miracle ointment works," she concluded.

The other horses did not improve nearly as much. Duke wondered why Tehachapi had fared better than the others had.

"My feet are still very tender, but better," Tehachapi told Nina. "Put some more of that miracle stuff on them and rub it in."

Poncho, who was the supervising the barn since Marty Torres had been injured, checked on Tehachapi. He said he would groom the horse himself until he was better.

"He's really important to the farm right now. Duke is under some pressure. Let me take care of him, so we can get him back to the races," said Poncho.

Poncho previously had been the head groom for trainer Hal Dryce for years at Santa Anita. Everyone respected him. He began working for Duke when Dryce closed his stable after Duke Snyder took over all of Tyler and Catrina Dovato's horses.

Poncho had integrated himself seamlessly into the barn, and had become a trusted member of the staff. He was one of the four who attended the summit at the ranch.

He took over as an assistant trainer at Santa Anita when Mr. Brown announced his semi-retirement. Scrap wanted to move back to Hollywood Park to work with Duke, and a majority of the horses. Poncho was elevated to the assistant's position, and Duke's winning percentages continued at high-level.

At the daylong meeting at the ranch after Marty's injury, everyone agreed a farm-racing manager was necessary. Immediately.

Duke would not be at the ranch every day. Angela worked with the young horses and rode too many others to manage the barn, as well. Torres was out of the equation.

"The best man for the responsible position is Poncho," Scrap suggested. Thereafter, he moved from Santa Anita temporarily to fill in. Everyone considered the success of the ranch vital.

Nina did not know Poncho well, but had been at the meeting. Certainly, she trusted Scrap. Most of all, Nina wanted to take care of her horse. Tehachapi was hers.

"Poncho, tell me what to do. I want to learn. I will follow instructions."

"Sometimes experienced hands on a horse are more important than merely instructing," Poncho said quietly. "We all want what is best for Tehachapi."

Nina did not argue.

Later, after Poncho and everyone had left the barn, Nina returned to Tehachapi's stall.

"How are the feet?"

"They hurt."

Nina, leg by leg, washed the feet. She dried them, and put the veterinarian's medical potion on each foot wrapping it—as she was taught by Scrap. She also checked Tehachapi's legs, back and withers.

"They are feeling better." Tehachapi reported, almost immediately.

"What is?"

"My feet are already feeling better. You rubbed the stuff in. I don't know. What you did, helped," said Tehachapi.

Nina reported to Angela her conversation with Tehachapi. Angela did not understand her niece's utterings to the horse, but she knew the young girl understood. She knew best what was going on with the colt.

"Nina has told me that Tehachapi was gimpy when she got to the barn this evening. She tended his feet again, and he is feeling better now. We all have total respect for Poncho, but I believe Nina is the best medicine for Tehachapi," Angela told Duke.

"Tehachapi is also the best medicine for Nina," he agreed. "However, I need Tehachapi to win at the track – especially now. The Racing Form has been critical. Despite that, we cannot crush her to win races. I'll tell everyone tomorrow that only Nina grooms Tehachapi. Give her guidance. Let her do the work."

The night air was cool, coming through the open window in Duke and Angela's room. They snuggled beneath the many blankets whispering stories of love in each other's ears.

Angela wanted in the worst way to have a baby. However, her mother had counseled, "Don't put any pressure on yourselves."

Her mother had continued, "Just, have fun with each other. If it takes a month or two or six months, enjoy the time. God knows best. Sometimes, he knows that a man and wife need time caressing each other. The better lover you are, the greater lover your husband will be."

Angela's mother had been correct when it took what seemed eons to Angela before Duke made his first move in their dating relationship. They had become close friends initially. After they won the Kentucky Derby with No Rain, they became lovers. Friends and lovers for life.

Now, the beautiful girl with the biggest brown eyes pulled Duke toward her.

"I need you. I need you – now. I love you." Nina said.

Duke did not say anything. His actions spoke louder than any words.

# Chapter 22

**More Leaks and Cracks.** Over the next two weeks, Tehachapi continued his miraculous recovery. He actually did not miss a day. His feet looked so much better on inspection by Duke; with the veterinarian's approval, the trainer dispensed putting pads on him.

With skillful hands, the veterinarian cut out two spots on Tehachapi's feet. Thereafter, Duke had mixed up a formula that Mr. Brown had taught him that included DSMO. The trainer put the ingredients in a frying pan bring it to a boil. Then, Duke let it simmer.

Tehachapi's feet were placed into the pan one at a time.

"This is called frying his feet," Duke explained.

"Uncle Duke, doesn't that hurt him?"

"To the contrary, the concoction is forced up. It both heals them and toughens them up," Duke instructed.

Tehachapi agreed, "He's right. My feet are feeling better and better."

Nina exclusively groomed the young colt. Many at the farm believed Poncho should be given the assignment. Ridiculous for a small fry to have the responsibility.

Duke resisted. "No, it is her horse. She works on him."

The Daily Racing Form reported, almost as if they had a bug in the colt's stall, recording conversations in the barn.

"Duke Snyder's talented distance runner, Tehachapi, is being groomed by a child. Duke refuses to administer treatment to the colt or to allow experienced farmhands to touch him."

Duke was irate and to the Form, demanding to know the source of their story. The Daily Racing Form refused.

"Are you denying that Nina Torres is the exclusive groom for Tehachapi?" the Form asked.

"As with every groom, I am ultimately responsible for the well-being of every animal. Nina has worked with Tehachapi since his birth. Before you write a story learn all the facts," he chided the publication.

"I can quote you as agreeing with our story that a child is grooming Tehachapi?"

"Certainly, I do not agree with the tenor of your story. The article should make the young feel confident they can work with animals. Check with our vet, and see how much Tehachapi has improved," Duke argued.

The damage done and Duke was losing owners. Tyler and Catrina Dovato were not leaving. Cory Bentley and other longtime Duke Snyder supporters stayed.

However, the floodgates open for the newer owners to leave. They could be as fickle as the latest rumor.

Another factor in the owners' frenzy was Duke's time away from Santa Anita and Hollywood Park. Duke felt his presence was necessary for Cummings Valley Ranch at the outset of the new program. His absence monitored daily by racing experts. There was no doubt Duke Snyder had developed a most dependable staff at the tracks. That went unreported.

Duke had always enjoyed an outstanding relationship with The Form; however, with the words that Duke exchanged, he was portrayed as a butcher. The Racing Form reported news daily on "the demise of the once unassailable Duke Snyder racing stable."

The trainer's win percentages actually increased over the period. Nevertheless, the winning percentage appeared in small print – almost as an afterthought.

Poncho caught up with Duke one the morning.

"Boss, don't you think it's time I go back to Santa Anita. It seems we need all our heavy hitters there right now. They are taking you apart. It's unfair. Nonetheless, that's what's happening."

"Angela and I believe you are a key part of our team. If we back down now, everyone will see I failed. Furthermore, everyone will know I'm a chicken. I need you here. When Marty Torres is better, maybe," Duke told the experienced hand.

"How is Marty doing?"

"Much better. We probably could rush him back in two or three weeks. The doctor says it will be better for him if we take six weeks," Duke explained.

Poncho said, "I'll do what's best for the stable. If you need me here, I'll be at the ranch until Marty is better."

The other colts injured with the rocks were slow to come around. Several two-year-olds experienced freak injuries and were lame. In all, racing from a ranch was not going as Duke had hoped.

"I'm going to have to spend more time at Hollywood Park and Santa Anita to quell the uprising," Duke reported to Angela.

"I'm going tomorrow morning for a couple of weeks," Duke said. "You and Poncho will have to hold the fort."

Angela asked, "Do you have second thoughts about racing from the farm?"

"I just don't know what to think right now. I need to clear my head."

The farm was uplifted that morning as Nina took her prized Tehachapi to the track. The two of them moved as one as they circled the half-mile oval.

"Tehachapi hasn't lost a step," Duke reported to Angela.

Nina let Tehachapi move on an extended gallop that took the two of them, a mile. The young horse did not take one bad step.

"I had him moving in 24 seconds a quarter. As soon as we can put air back into him, he'll be ready to run," Duke said.

### At Hollywood Park – Early.

Bedlam surrounded the barn as Duke Snyder walked into his stable at Hollywood Park. There were owners milling around, reporters, and other people who did not seem to have any reason to be there.

Scrap had magical hands when placed on horses. Other grooms followed him as a leader, because they could see the results of his actions. He was soft-spoken. Scrap never raised his voice. He did not argue with people, but pulled them along with respect.

Nonetheless, when things fell apart, and there was screaming instead of adulation, Scrap added little. He had no stomach for infighting, backbiting, and revolt.

Duke stopped short, just inside the barn entrance, where he could observe the calamity.

Owners were actually climbing into the horse enclosures and inspecting their animals. Although every one of the owners had money – some were rich – none of them had the slightest idea what was right and what was wrong with any horse.

Scrap said nothing. Mr. Brown, who had more experience at the track than many of the owners had been alive, worked quietly with an animal. Many of the other grooms were standing aside afraid to be combative.

Duke entered into the center aisle, among the revolting parties. He stood tall and quiet. One by one, the interlopers saw him. His physical presence stopped them without a word.

"Hold it. Owners, get the hell out of the stalls. If you are not an owner, get the hell out of my barn. Now," said Duke sternly, but without raising his voice.

Within seconds, there was not an owner in a horse box. Without a word, the non-owners departed unceremoniously. The reporters from the Daily Racing Form did not ask a question. They had their story – Duke Snyder was back.

"I don't know what the hell is going on here, but it's over."

One of the owners, a prominent attorney in a large Los Angeles law firm, took offense.

"You can't talk to me that way. We have a right to know what's going on with our horses."

"You're quite correct; you have the absolute right to know what is going on with your animals. If anyone of you had asked Scrap quietly, he would have spent an hour with you telling you every aspect."

Duke continued, after a short pause, "If anyone of you had picked up the phone and called me on my cell – you all have the number – I would have filled you in. None of you have the right to demean the personnel at my barn or climb into stalls risking injury to you or the horses."

Duke quietly walked over to his office, and pulled out some folding chairs.

He sat them down in a semi-circle. Without a word, he sat. A number of the owners followed suit, sitting in the chairs facing each other. Some of the more combative forces put their noses to the air, and left the barn and a huff.

"First, I want to apologize to all of you. I should have spent more time explaining," Duke said humbly.

He spent half an hour telling the inquisitive group about the mother's rampage at Cummings Valley, and the two children left without a shoulder to cry on. He also confessed his deep and abiding love for Angela, and his desire to have children of his own.

"I won't let anything go wrong with your horses."

Duke explained in detail how horses trained in other parts of the world. He said animals at the track spend twenty-three hours a day in a stall. At a farm, there are provisions for turnouts where horses can eat grass, lay in the sun, and the horses can have a life.

"In a way, it is a prison here for the animals."

Some of the owners started to nod. Others seemed unconvinced.

"I believe it's been proven that many horses are happier and run better under those conditions. Some horses that might be great are lost at the track, because they can't tolerate twenty-three hours a day in a horse stall."

An owner asked, "Are you taking our horses to the farm?"

"No. I am working out the hard details with my own animals and at my expense. Not one of your animals will go to the farm, unless we sit down and talk about it first. You will have to be the judge of whether my horses run well from the farm."

Attorney Cory Bentley, who was Duke's oldest client, walked in. Put a hand on the back of one of the seated owners.

"Hey Cory. Going to join us?" the owner asked.

"Sure. Duke, good to see you're still alive," said Cory in a friendly banter. "Thought you might be lynched — I could pick up a new criminal case here today," he said lightly. The twosome had always joked with each other.

"Pull up a chair," Duke invited. "Cory has spent some time in England, and can tell you the methods used by some famous trainers."

Bentley, who made his life convincing people his clients were innocent in famous criminal trials, came to Duke's defense. He eloquently explained how trainers for centuries had work from home, with stables called "yards," where they prepared their runners.

Little by little, Duke noticed the grooms were silently tending their horses. Scrap was inspecting animals as they came out of each stall. Exercise riders mounted the horses and took them out for exercise.

"Let me conclude by saying, I believe in the staff. I think our record of achievement bears out my faith in them. I would think now that I have shed myself of training horses in the East, you as owners would be fortified. Know I can oversee the remaining horses here and at Santa Anita."

Looking around, Duke continued, "If anyone desires to change trainers, I will understand. There will not be acrimony. Call me and we will do it face-to-face with a handshake. That's a promise."

With that, the Hollywood Park revolt was abated. Over the next two days, fourteen horses left the barn, all of them from the owners who stormed out without meeting with Duke.

Later, that evening, Duke, Cory Bentley, Catrina Dovato, Catrina's father and Duke's friend Tony, as well as two other major farm owners had dinner at the Velvet restaurant. It was a meeting of friends.

"Well, give us a report," said Cory Bentley. "How many horses did you lose?"

"I'd rather talk about the horses that remain, and my friends here at this dinner," Duke said earnestly. "My report to you my Board of Directors..."

Everyone laughed, because this was a meeting of friends – not a Board of Directors meeting.

"We have a hundred and twelve horses at Hollywood Park and Santa Anita. Seventeen are stake's winners. Seventy-one are two-year-olds. The remainders are winners. Not bad for a barn in disarray," Duke joked.

### Not backing down.

Three days later Duke entered horses in all nine races on the Hollywood Park card. The stake's race that day was only for $75,000.

However, the astonishing event was viewing Duke's horses winning every single race that Wednesday afternoon. No other trainer ever accomplished such a feat.

Three of the races were for maidens; two races for two-year-old allowance horses, and three races for medium priced claiming horses. Perhaps, it was the luck of the draw. Nonetheless, Duke had outstanding contenders for each division. He stacked the deck.

A reporter for the Daily Racing Form asked Duke for a comment following the concluding event.

"Winning every race on a card is a testament to the training staff, including Scrap, the wonderfully experienced grooms, and hot walkers. Moreover, the exercise riders. Furthermore, I think it helps that jockeys Joe Calamos and Nettie work the horses in the morning.

The tide turned.   A number of owners approached Duke about taking their horses.   Duke told everyone, "We aren't taking new owners right now.  We are working on making our barn the best it can be, as well as sorting out how to train from our ranch.  If you're still interested in a couple of months, check back with us."

Refusing to accept new owners became a flash around the track. When you told a moneyed owner, they could not have something – they had to have it.

Moreover, The Daily Racing Form backed down.  They wrote a genuine story with pictures of the great No Rain, No Rainbows, and others who achieved from Duke's barn.

"It is clear this established trainer is striving for new heights on a path never before taken in America.  Will it work?  Only time will tell," the Form said.

"But the new path is being taken with caution.  Duke is a very organized and loving trainer," they wrote.

### Meanwhile, Tehachapi Strikes at Cummings Valley

With Duke at Hollywood Park, Poncho took absolute control at the farm.

In the morning – after Tehachapi had galloped a strong three miles – Poncho announced to Angela, he was going to survey the colt's legs and feet.  Nina was at school, so she could not protest.

"Wouldn't it be better to wait until Nina returns this afternoon?" Angela asked, as Poncho prepared to enter the two-year-olds stall.

"No, I think it's best I have a look without her interference.  She's a child.  What does she know?"

Angela bit her tongue.  She was furious, but understood the ranch could ill afford to lose its assistant trainer while Duke was away.

Poncho took out an elongated hoof pick and knife combination, and entered my horse stall.

'He thought I wasn't looking," thought Tehachapi.  "I was looking out the rear window with my back to the webbing."

I saw the man with the knife.

"Now, for you," said Poncho in a low gruff voice. "My time to fix you."

I intentionally waited until the man was in the stall, and was kneeling with the knife pointed toward me.

"Does this idiot of a groom think I'm a fool?" Tehachapi said to himself.

Poncho moved to nick Tehachapi's tendon. The injury would ruin the young horse for racing.  The man menacingly jabbed.

"Remember, clod, I am not fast...but I am extremely quick."

I saw it coming.  I sidestepped Poncho, moving my front foot left – away from him.

"Now we'll see if you can keep up, clown," I said to him— knowing he did not understand me. He wasn't as smart as my Nina.

I planted my rear legs toward the side of the stall closest to him.

"The exit is now blocked, you murdering bum. The front of the stall is cut off."

The move blocked the groom in the box with no quick retreat. The horsebox was larger than most; however, I cut off the ring in the parlance of a great boxer.

"Are you thinking, you are going to play with me?" asked Poncho, a killer's look on his face.

"Damned right," I said, knowing he was deaf to me. I understood both his intent and his words. Advantage — little ole me – the horse, born too small that no one wanted.

This jerk must think I am an ignoramus. He thinks I am going to let him cripple me without fighting back. Not a chance. I thought quickly.

The dance was on. Clearly, I was the orchestrator as I bumped and pushed Poncho around the stall. He is my rag doll.

I knock him down five straight times without injury to me. Then, he got in a good lick with his knife high on my shoulder.

"Ok, Ali," I said to myself, "Do the shuffle quicker."

The knife stung as it slipped into my sleek colt. My long mane helped protect me from the blade going deep.

Until then, I was just warding off this creature, trying to knock him off his feet until he decided to run. However, once it was clear he came to kill me, my intent darkened.

"Got you — you rat bastard," he screamed.

"Last time."

"Now, I'm going to cut through your pastern. You won't even be able to limp. Not waddle like that gimp of a girl."

I thought, "Wonderful man, this Poncho. So great to have him here with our family."

Seeing that he had drawn blood, Poncho became bolder. He held the knife out in front of him, with his feet separated in a fighting stance.

The ruckus caused barn workers to rush to Tehachapi's stall, including Angela.

At first, it appeared Tehachapi was the unwieldy creature.

"Tehachapi's trying to kill Poncho. He's gone mad," screamed a female worker.

An onlooker believed, Poncho was merely protecting himself. Tehachapi cornered off the stall; there was no easy exit for the assistant trainer.

"He's trying to kill me," yelled Poncho. "He's kicked me several times already," he lied.

Angela yelled, "Tehachapi stop." Normally, I obeyed flawlessly. However, it was clear this was no ordinary event.

I said to myself, "Stop before he drops the knife. If I do, it's curtains for me."

Poncho lunged at me again with the knife in the menacing position. At the same time, Poncho appeared as if he was trying to make flight from the stall. In fact, he was trying to cut me from the chest to my rear.

I saw him coming, and made a quick wielding turn. My rear legs were near him. I found him leaning in. Still wielding the knife.

"Mistake," I said. "Bad mistake."

With one savage kick, I caught him on his upper arm. The blow flung him like a rag doll against the side of the box.

I was not taking any chances with this coward. I moved into a striking position. Nonetheless, I did not attack; nor did I retreat.

"Get a pitchfork, and kill him," ordered Poncho, groggily as he climbed to his feet.

Angela countermanded the order.

"Forget that nonsense, Poncho get the hell out of the stall."

The assistant trainer lost his knife in my rear leg kick. However, he went berserk. Rather than retreating, Poncho lurched at me swinging his fists.

This was no challenge. Even if he had connected, it would not have done damage to me. Nevertheless, I have had enough.

"Timber," I said — regaining my sense of humor.

I took one swift kick to his stomach. I did not plant it with all my heart. My rear legs were not the mightiest, but a kick to his solar plexus, while he was moving toward me, put him down on all four gasping for air.

"Fight over. I'm the winner. No need to count him out – he is done."

Everyone, including Angela, was afraid to enter my stall. They believed I had gone mad. I turned toward Angela and moved to the webbing. I put my head-down low, so she could pat it.

"I talked to her, but she did not understand."

As I faced forward, I had an eye on the villain behind. If he climbed to his feet, I would plant him again.

"Are you okay, boy?" asked Angela, petting me.

"Yes," I said, nodding my head.

Angela appeared to understand, because she opened the webbing. Now, she came in without hesitation. She had another groom help Poncho from my stall.

They remembered the stories about the great Man-Of-War. He was accused of killing grooms. I do not know the whole story; I only know what Nina has told me.

As I understand it, Man-Of-War finally found a kind man. Be it, he drank too much. The groom watched over the stallion until his death. The groom slept most nights in Man-of-War's stall.

"Would there be stories that I am a killer?"

"Tehachapi's been injured," announced Tillie, a young girl who fed and watered the horses.

Angela tended to Poncho, telling him to take the rest of the day off. She called the doctor.

"Let me see," said Angela coming into my stall. Any impartial observer knew I was friendly. I let Tillie come in and examine me. If Nina were not at home, Angela would be my second choice to clean and bandage my wound.

"Tillie, go call the vet. Tell him that Tehachapi has been cut," ordered Angela. She wondered what had really set the two off against each other.

"I would tell her if she listened with her heart," I thought.

### More News to the Form

More news scorched the Daily Racing Form. The headlines screamed assistant trainer savaged by Tehachapi, as the horse goes mad. The newspaper reported a one-sided account. The question was, where did they get their facts?

The old story says, "Say what you want, just spell my name correct." Tehachapi was becoming a legend. He won a stake's race in his first outing. He was taken unceremoniously to a remote ranch in the mountains. Story after story came from the small village town.

One-story told of a young girl who was exclusively grooming the horse. The next review told that an experienced groom was savaged by this killer two-year-old colt.

"Doesn't make sense," said one reader. "There is something between the lines we are not being told."

What was the truth? No one knew. Tehachapi was the gossip of the turf world.

I did not care for the reports I heard. My Nina got the truth out of me when she returned from school. However, no one really believed her, because she was so obviously one-sided in my favor.

Poncho demanded to go back to the track. Duke told him to stay out of my stall, and that they would work out things when Duke returned to Cummings Valley Ranch.

Nina said, "Dad says you have to watch your step. If you get a reputation as a mad horse it will be tough on you when you go to the track."

"It's not my fault."

"Quit being defensive. Take it as a challenge."

"Just keep Poncho out of my stall.'

Nina said, "Don't give him a chance to come in. Do not eat anything that I don't fix for you. We've got to be certain you are not poisoned."

"I thought this was supposed to be the great life?" I said to her.

"Who told you that this is heaven?" countered the little girl with so much sense.

# Chapter 23

**A Murder without Explanation**. Poncho returned the next day full of good cheer. Reading his expression, everyone still believed I, the loser horse, had the murderous intent. I was the plague.

"I have no idea why Tehachapi turned on me. I've always been so kind to him," Poncho said. "I guess he's a one-person horse. There are some dogs that turn vicious when anyone except their owner handles them."

The farm workers genuinely liked Poncho. He was kind and generous to them. He taught them real skills, from his lifetime at the racetrack. Therefore, everyone assumed I was a villain.

I used to get carrots – now I get grumbles. I used to get pats – now, people walk around my stall.

Old man Tom Fryers worked tirelessly on the track. He was retired, but you would not know it from the effort he put into the racing surface.

There was a clear improvement. Nina questioned me about how my legs and feet felt on the track surface.

"When I go over it each day, it feels like silk. Even when Nina's dad cared for the track, it might look good, but it was rough, too compact, and abrasive to my feet."

Fryers tilled topsoil into the blend, which held the track together throughout the day.

"Maybe you should be an advisor to tracks; help them prepare their course," complimented Angela.

Poncho said, "The horses are coming back better, Tom."

Everyone believed the farm was turning the corner, and Duke's racing plans might be possible. The next morning, Angela woke up with a smile on her face. Nina knew innately that her uncle was heading home.

"Uncle Duke must be home she told me. Angela is floating off the ground as you do when you race," said the observant youth.

Duke rose early and had pancakes with the family, including Marty and Mary. Angela explained that Mary had started staying in Marty's small ranch home, abandoning her beautiful abode to be with him.

"Women and their love make happy homes, not property," reflected the trainer — looking into Marty's eyes. Clearly, he was sending a message — man to man.

It was a cold December morning, but the birds appeared to be singing. Duke and Angela were caught kissing in the kitchen. Moments later Tommy found Marty kissing Mary under the mistletoe in the living room.

The children feigned embarrassment over the passions of the adults, but secretly love and affection had been scarce in their young lives.

Nina especially believed this was going to be a good Christmas. "Before, Christmas had always been depressing," she told me.

"And I thought Christmas celebrated Jesus' life — not yours," Tehachapi scolded.

"As I've told you, Jesus is an everyday subject. He should be in our hearts. If there is depression all around, it is hard to capture his loving message. Yes, Christmas does celebrate his birthday."

Nina smiled. A confident smile, seldom seen in holidays past.

"Love is all around. Beauty begets beauty." Nina said.

"Oh, my goodness, you're becoming a poet."

"Not so. Nonetheless, I'm feeling love at home."

After breakfast, everybody, including Marty and Mary made their way to the big green monster barn. They joined hands on a walk to Tehachapi's stall. However, before they ever got there, Angela noticed cows grazing on the racetrack.

"Duke, look," she said, pointing at the track. "Cows are wandering onto the track."

The party diverted their trip and found more than thirty head, tearing up the track. The outer rail and fence were cut. No doubt— intentionally.

"No permanent damage," said Duke. "But you were just telling me how perfect the track was. Now, we're going to have to spend a couple of hours making repairs before we can work the horses."

"Where's old man Fryers?" Angela asked. "He's the man who can make it right."

"He's hardly in retirement as hard as he works on the surface." Duke reported accurately.

They were surprised the old man was not working; normally, Fryers appeared at the track at daybreak. He would til and get it ready, so the horses could train first thing in the morning.

Around ten a.m., Fryers would water and re-work the track for the horses breezing that day. Afterwards, his day was over.

Fryers would come out again in early evening, and add additional soil into the track. Water it lightly preparing for the next morning.

"Yes, where is he?" Nina agreed. "He is always here."

When the old man was not present and cows were meandering over his precious racing surface, everyone became concerned.

"I can take the cart; go get him at his bunkhouse," said Marty. "It will give me an excuse not to have to bend over the horses quite yet."

Mary, giving him a kiss, said she would ride along with him.

Tom Fryers lived in a one-room, four hundred square foot bunkhouse. He told everyone he loved it. It was his. Fryers had constructed an old potbelly stove – fireplace, which warmed his home.

Mary and Marty parked the four-person cart. They held hands as they strolled up the path to Fryer's house, with rose bushes on each side of the path.

"These flowers are going to be spectacular come spring," said Mary, who loved nature almost as she did her man. They were not in bloom at this time of the year, but clear Tom planted them, planning to stay forever.

"Oh my God," cried Mary after she opened the door. Blood was everywhere. Tom Fryers' body was on the floor with a knife stuck in his chest. It was quickly apparent—Tom had been stabbed many times.

"Murder," mouthed Marty, truly unable to speak.

On the wall, written in blood was "Death to Duke."

"Who could have hated this kind-hearted man?" Marty Torres asked. "All he did was spread kindness."

It was clear Tom Fryers had not died quickly as blood squirted on the walls and floor. The bunkhouse had a four-foot tall Christmas tree at one end of the room with Christmas presents wrapped neatly. When he died, Tom was wrapping presents for everyone at the ranch.

"I'm no detective; Tom knew his killer that is for certain," Marty said with difficulty.

Mary looked down and saw presents to Nina, Tommy, Angela, Poncho, Tillie and other workers.

"He worked and he spent his money, making things better for others."

Duke and Angela were summoned to Tom Fryers' home. When the sheriff arrived, Duke said he had no explanation for the murder.

"This man was given retirement here. He chose to work, because he loved the people and the farm."

Tears rolled down Angela's face.

"I don't have a suspect. None at all," Duke told the officers. "We have had some unexplained skullduggery around here, but nothing like this."

"Could it have something to do with the shootings of that crazy lady Cheri? You know the one that went on a rampage."

"No. Tom was not involved with her. He didn't even know her."

Duke walked slowly from Tom's abode. He thought, what was Nina saying – "Love is all around?"

# Chapter 24

**Buried Treasure**. Three days after Tom's death, we were back at work at Cummings Valley Ranch. Everyone dismal; Tom was family to us and everyone to him.

No one understood why Duke appointed Poncho as the new track superintendent. Clearly, he was much more adept at helping hands learn the trade of grooming horses.

Pancho, also, was responsible for the soundness of every horse in the barn.

"As a racing stable, we are not going further than the condition of our track. Tom Fryer began our journey – now Poncho will take us home," Duke pronounced at a meeting of the entire farm ranch personnel.

"The track is the key."

"Right you are," said Pancho.

Pancho said it was a great honor; however, again requested to be relieved so he could return home to Santa Anita.

"I can do more in one day there than in a month here. Give me Tehachapi; we'll win the Santa Anita Derby. He will stay sound for years there."

"Appreciate the offer. Now – especially at the moment — we need you here," the headman replied.

Marty and Mary were assigned temporarily as assistant trainers. Mary was pinch-hitting. Marty asked to watch – not do the actual work.

"I don't understand," said Poncho. "Have I done something wrong?"

"No. Why would you ask? The track has to be perfect. You're the man," said Duke.

It was clear Pancho was upset at the assignment. He agreed the track was the most important; nevertheless, he did not want the job. He felt he could make a bigger contribution at Santa Anita. This farm was not The Great Race Place.

"He had been marked by anxious uneasiness since being sent to the ranch from his previous post at Santa Anita," Angela thought. "Almost don't recognize him. Before, he was on the same trusted level as Scrap."

Angela, Marty and even Scrap asked Duke if he had lost his mind with the new assignment. Scrap called Duke from Hollywood Park, asking that Poncho be sent to Santa Anita or Hollywood Park immediately.

"He's the best of the best grooming at a race track," Scrap confided.

"I've got him where I need him," Duke responded.

No one understood.

Training normally started with the first gallopers reaching the track by 7:45 a.m. However, Duke held the exercisers from going to the track each morning.

Duke would take his pony horse, Momentum, out for a morning stroll on the track. With a bottle of diet Coke, Momentum and Duke would wander around the oval. It did not appear Duke was paying attention to anything.

"Are you okay?" everyone asked.

"He's taking Tom's death badly," Angela explained.

Once he returned to the barn, Angela and the other riders would get the string out. Late—but out.

"Honey, what in the hell is going on. We're losing an hour or more each day with you meandering," Angela criticized.

The next day, the same thing. Duke and Momentum riding aimlessly around the track. That day Duke returned and saddled his old pony horse, Tough Stuff, and made another jaunt.

Angela could not get the string out until 10 a.m.

"We can't afford to lose two hours each day."

Angela knew her husband. She knew he had not lost his mind. Certainly, he was upset with the death of Tom, but she had seen him handle adversity. He appeared almost manic to her – and to the training staff.

The next morning Duke feigned illness. He did not appear for his morning track therapy. Angela instructed that four horses be saddled, and ready to go for the first set in "ten minutes."

Angela took the lead and instructed the set to ride two-by-two. This instruction meant that two horses would be side-by-side, and an additional team followed the leaders.

"Outside of the track. Keep the inside clear for workers," she instructed.

Every time Angela rode, there was grace in the saddle. She was a rare beauty. As the horses played follow the leader, Angela kept them away from where horses would breeze a half mile on the racetrack. No one questioned her instructions. The horses galloped a mile and returned to the barn.

Poncho moved over and held a newly broken two-year-old for Angela.

"Any workers this morning?" Poncho asked, confirming what he was told the night before.

"Yes, Tehachapi is going to work a mile right after this set. That's why I'm keeping to the outside of the track. I wanted the surface perfect for him," Angela replied.

"Sure. Makes sense."

Angela took the next group of four horses twice around the half-mile track without incident.

"Let's get Tehachapi ready to go one mile," Angela instructed.

"Nina is not here. Who's going to hold him?" a groom asked. People were still afraid of the Tehachapi myth.

"I will," volunteered Mary.

"I'm a gimp. So, I will saddle him," said Marty. Everyone laughed.

All the ranch grooms wanted to see little dynamite work a mile, so the barn emptied as Angela brought Tehachapi out onto the track.

"I'm going to warm him up in the open paddock, so he doesn't get too high before his work," Angela explained.

This was somewhat unusual, but everyone thought it might be a good idea.

Poncho, learning that his nemesis Tehachapi was indeed working that morning, had moved from the barn. He was standing on the viewing riser on the far side of the track. Most of the workers spread along the railing nearest the barn.

After Angela warmed Tehachapi, and was heading toward the track, Duke's cart sprang from a location near his home. It was clear, even though Duke appeared to be sick, he did not want to miss the Little Giant's work.

Instead of meandering toward the viewing stand or another vantage point on the rail, Duke drove his cart onto the track. Simultaneously, farm members noticed sheriff vehicles emerging from the far end of the ranch.

"What's going on?" Mary asked.

Marty shrugged. "No idea."

"Duke has snared a mouse in his trap; I imagine," Angela explained. He is about the best detective, there is. If he stopped training tomorrow, he could make a great living detecting."

Duke wielded his cart to a portion of the track across from where Poncho was standing. He parked, climbed out, and surveyed the racing surface. Observing Duke's intent, Poncho retreated quickly from the viewing stand, and started to make his way to his vehicle.

"Going somewhere?" said a sergeant grabbing Poncho's arm.

"Take your hands off of me. I haven't done anything," Poncho demanded.

The officer took the squirming, so-called track superintendent into custody.

It did not take Duke three minutes to uncover the metal treachery Poncho had planted in the Cummings Valley Ranch track. The device stretched about five feet out under the surface; buried under a soft cushion top layer of soil.

"When a horse stepped on the device, lights out."

Nina and Angela advised Duke of Poncho's combat with Tehachapi at the time of the barn incident. The trainer understood the horse's temperament; knew immediately Tehachapi had not thrown a temper tantrum. When Tom Fryers was murdered, all the pieces fit.

"Click."

It was as if television's Monk was at Cummings Valley. Duke knew for certain Poncho had murdered Tom. However, he had no proof.

Duke baited the trap by insisting Poncho become track superintendent. He realized the experienced assistant trainer had taken it as a snub when removed as number one in command at Santa Anita. The insult of being forced to the farm made him snap.

"It didn't matter how nice a home he would be provided. It didn't matter how much he would be paid."

The trainer realized Poncho was in the perfect position to feed the Daily Racing Form hateful information. Furthermore, Duke saw how Poncho sabotaged the horses, including Tehachapi.

"Over here. We are going to have to dig down and pull this out. Take pictures first," Duke instructed. "I took plenty with a long lens when Pancho buried it.

Marty came over and saw the trap had been set to snare Tehachapi.

"How did you know where it was?"

"I watched with an 800 mm lens and my trusty Canon camera, as he planted it."

Marty suggested getting the tractor. "We should dig down a good foot to be sure no other death waits."

"I don't think there is, but it won't hurt," Duke agreed. "Marty, before you dig up the track, I want you to study it. If it takes a day, it is okay. Old man Fryers knew what he was doing. I don't think Poncho had time to ruin it."

"I agree. I can learn from Tom. I'll take my time, and when I say go, it will be safe," Marty said.

Tehachapi galloped through Cummings Valley that day – he did not breeze.

"Duke is a wonder," Tehachapi thought. "He is quiet, loving, and understanding. It is no wonder all of his horses try so hard to win. I know I am going to do my best for him. He just saved my life."

It took about thirty minutes of forceful questioning before Poncho cracked – broke down.

"I've spent my life building up a reputation at the Great Race Place. Duke Snyder comes along and expects me to teach to degenerates at a farm? I told him I wanted to go back to Santa Anita. I told him every day. He humiliated me," Poncho confessed.

"Why didn't you simply quit?"

"I've never quit anything."

"Murder is better??

Pancho said nothing.

There was no question Poncho had contributed mightily to Duke Snyder, and other racing stables for three decades. Perhaps, it was an insult to ask a man of his stature to come to Cummings Valley Ranch.

"Tom Fryers spent his life working with horses at Hollywood Park. We invited him to come with us, and he thrived," Duke said.

Angela countered, "Yes, but he was retired. He wanted to come. He wanted a new home. Poncho wanted to be at Santa Anita running a barn."

"That is a reason to kill a prince of a man?" Duke asked.

# Chapter 25

**The Little Giants Works.** I am still a little runt. By the standards horsemen use to pick horses in the million-dollar bidding arenas in Kentucky, I am worth nothing. I have flashbacks to my early days here at the farm, where I was a loser.

"I couldn't imagine all the happenings at our farm. Murders, laming of horses, and blaming Duke for innovation."

It took three days for Marty to push the track back together. We had a day of rain, but Tom Fryer's track mixture held together during the downfall. Duke had taken Momentum over it this morning and pronounced it safe and "wonderful."

It was Saturday, the best day of the week, because Nina was home. In a couple of weeks, she would have vacation time for the Christmas holiday, which would make the days even better. For now, I was thankful she was ready to ride me this morning.

With everything that had gone on, I still had put in the miles. Nina and I rode like the wind. Sometimes the bigger the wind – whether it be from personal problems at home – or the inclemency of the weather, we rode further.

Duke was intent on seeing where my condition stood. He wanted Nina to breeze me a mile and gallop out until I got tired.

What Uncle Duke still had not learned the further I went, the better, I liked it? A mile was a mere warm-up. "I found myself calling him uncle now, as well."

"How do you feel? How are the legs? How fast should we go today?" Nina was happy.

Marty and Mary were in love, which breathed fresh air into her heart.

"I'm great," I reported. "It's obvious you're better."

"Yep. I guess we are going home to Mary's house. I am going to get my own room. She says I can decorate my way." She was all smiles, shaking at times from the excitement. "My own room."

Nina was absent-minded that morning, a condition that I did not recognize. My friend was hopeful of having a mother, a faithful companion; she could talk to and rely on. I am happy for my friend. She has suffered so much.

Once Nina climbed aboard, we were one. There was not me, and there wasn't her – there was only us.

We backtracked away on Marty Torres's track, which felt spongy and soft underfoot.

"He had learned the secrets of an old man, who died for us here in Cummings Valley."

We both felt there were no longer traitors at the farm. You could actually feel the love. No one could be around Angela and not feel her heart go out to her husband. And now, Mary and Marty found their way home.

We got to the viewing stand where Duke stood.

"How fast are you guys going this morning?"

"How fast is fast?" Nina responded. "Tehachapi can go twenty-four seconds a quarter forever. Is that what you want?"

Duke responded, "You've been on him. Without harm, what's he ready to do?"

"Why don't I work him within himself, and ask him the final quarter. I will let him jog out."

Duke looked at his niece in amazement. No child her age should understand the concept of working a horse within himself. Many experienced exercise riders never grasp the concept. Some jockeys failed to understand it their entire career.

"Sounds great."

Nina piloted me back to the starting line. We picked up the pace. We were clicking off just better than twelve seconds every eighth of a mile.

Frankly, I am not fast. Any sprinter can annihilate me. I can run 24 seconds a quarter mile. Forever. Horse breeders have bred endurance out of the modern horse racing in an attempt to gain the fastest animal. Sprinters can run one minute eight seconds for six furlongs.

"Anything over a mile, horses start to slush along as if they are pulling a sleigh."

It was good to stretch our legs again. It had been a while since Nina and I had opened up the accelerator. After we went a complete lap, Duke yelped over his megaphone we had completed the half-mile course in 47 2/5 seconds.

"Easy as pie," I sighed.

"Another lap, same pace," said Nina.

I started to pick up the fractions, but she sent me a clear message broadcast through the reins. There was no tug. She now possessed a quiet expertise. Nina held the reins firmly without the slightest movement.

"Yet, she told me. Told me firmly what she expected. She was the boss, so I followed instructions."

As we were heading into the final turn, I felt a slight tremble from her leg with a brace, which told me that she was tiring. She steadied herself with her knees bent inward for support. I knew that hurt her.

Almost at once, Nina gently shook the reins at me. I sprang into instant action. I was allowed to run a little more than an eighth of a mile to the wire, before Nina wrapped up on me. I expected we would gallop out another two laps of our track.

However, after one complete circle at a fair clip, Nina pulled me up.

When we were back at the barn, Duke joined us as Nina was helped from my back.

"I'm sorry Uncle Duke; we only galloped out half-mile, but my bad leg was extremely tired."

Duke wrapped Nina in his arms, telling her how proud he was of her.

"Many riders would have pushed beyond their limits and fallen; you adjusted the work to complete it safely."

Marty and Angela joined, with Marty asking, "How fast was the mile?"

Duke held out his stopwatch with the clocking 1:34 2/5.

"Wow."

"A bit fast?" Angela conjectured. "Especially, on a half-mile track."

Duke was silent. Normally, his demeanor would instantaneously show the rider, whether the horse had gone too fast.

"I would say Tehachapi did it totally within himself. Nina only asked him for a little more than an eighth of a mile."

Nina chipped in, "I was the one who got tired. I'm not used to going that fast. I need to strengthen my legs, if I'm going to help out."

Taking Tehachapi's reigns, Angela knelt next to me and felt my legs. I knew before her gentle touch that I was fine. Nina and I only went at a steady pace.

"His tendons are as tight as can be," she pronounced.

"Feel me," Nina said. "I'm the one that is shaking. I need to get on more horses that are working, so I can strengthen my legs," she said with resolve.

Angela asked, "What's next for Tehachapi?"

"With all that has gone on, I believe we must obtain a registered work at Hollywood Park before we run him. I want Angela to gallop him two miles every day for five days. Next, we will ship him to the track for a work," Duke said.

A wry smile crept onto the trainer's face. Everyone saw it. However, it needed translation. Even Angela did not have a clue. Duke was becoming the man of mystery.

"It must be big," she knew.

# Chapter 26

**The Storks on the Way.** Christmas lights were everywhere. Cummings Valley ranch decorated to the hilt. The staff asked if the farm was expecting visitors to inspect the two-year-olds.

"Is that the reason for all the lights?"

Merriment washed across the hearts of those who worked at the farm. Only a month earlier there despair clung heavy here in the mountains; now there was resolve.

The two-year-olds were clicking along under Angela's trained eye. Marty Torres returned as assistant manager. It was quite evident that Mary was in love, and that her heart included the children.

Nina took on a strengthening program vigorously. Doctors had urged her to undergo physical therapy. Now, she did it with a purpose.

Nina and I went on an open two-mile extended gallop on the track five days after our work. This time Nina glued to me without a bobble.

"Tehachapi and I flew like the eagle," she told Duke over the telephone. The trainer was flying to Hollywood Park three days a week. He would arrive early for works in the morning, stay for the races and saddle winners, and return in the evening.

That afternoon Angela and Mary were huddled in the vet room inside the barn. They were talking as chattering hens do. Both were quite excited.

The two were about the same age and had a great deal in common. They were very much sisters.

The Cummings Valley Ranch inner circle was growing together in a closely-knit family.

"I'm pregnant."

Just as the words were spoken, Marty Torres was walking into the vet room to pick up supplies. He heard "pregnant."

He had not heard who said them.

Marty staggered slightly, approaching the chattering twosome and said to Mary, "You're what?"

Mary winked with her right eye at Angela. Marty could not see her wink. So, the two played him.

"Aren't you excited?" Mary asked Marty.

Already, the father of two children, and just recently getting his feet under him since his relationship with Mary had blossomed, Marty stood frozen for a moment.

"Yes," he said in a strong voice.

The joke was on Mary. She expected him to run as most men do when they think they are to be a father and are unmarried.

Mary knew for certain, without a centimeter of doubt, Marty Torres loved her. He loved her unconditionally.

Angela had to confess to her brother that Duke was going to be the proud papa.

"You better keep your mouth shut until I can tell him properly. You weren't supposed to hear me confiding to my sister."

"Sister?" asked Marty confused. He did not get it.

"Men," said Mary laughing.

At home, Angela decorated their bedroom with storks hanging from the ceiling, a bassinet on the end of the bed, and a giant red heart, with "I love you," written in white letters in the center of it.

That evening, Duke said he was going to turn in early because he was tired, and went to the bedroom alone. Inside the room, he stood frozen for a second. A moment later, he bounded out looking for his bride.

Quietly, Angela followed him up the stairs. She met him outside the double-door entrance to their bedroom.

"I love you." She patted her stomach, and rushed to him – jumping into his arms.

Duke caught off guard. He tumbled backward. Even then, he was able to catch Angela and maintain his balance. He gave her a good old-fashioned kiss.

Then they retired for the evening to seal the deal.

"More whispering tonight, huh?" She kidded.

# Chapter 27

**History in the Making.** Following the script, Duke planned Tehachapi' training meticulously. The colt would turn three-years-old on New Year's Day, and clearly the barn favorite. He was trucked to Hollywood Park two days before his scheduled breeze.

"You guys are coming with me," he had said to his entire family that morning.

Unexpectedly, Angela and Nina accompanied Duke when he flew into Los Angeles International Airport. Duke kept his twin-engine jet at Vance Aviation, which was on the opposite side from the passenger terminals.

Duke had not explained anything to Nina about why she was going. She was excited. Nina was happy she was going to be on hand to watch her friend work.

When Duke, Angela and Nina walked into the Snyder Racing Stable, there was a buzz afloat. It was not similar to the disaster ongoing when Duke arrived with the owners in the horse boxes. This was excitement – not acrimony.

"What is happening?" Nina wondered.

She saw Tehachapi walking with Scrap in the center of the stall area. She raced to him and gave him a hug.

"Missed you, Tehachapi."

I told her I missed her too. I asked Nina about the fuss. I did not understand. Many owners were turning out today. Way more than normal.

The Daily Racing Form had a reporter, and even other trainers were milling around. Crazy, I thought.

"What is going on?" I asked her.

We did not have long to wait.  Duke instructed Angela to hoist Nina on Tehachapi's back.

"What. I get to ride, Tehachapi?" Nina asked.

Angela nodded her head.  Almost immediately, Nina saw Marty and Mary come out of the office.  Obviously, there had been a well-executed secret.

Duke untied his track pony horse, Charging Home, and climbed aboard.

"I've arranged with the stewards, that you can show your riding prowess this morning.  I've explained that you ride Tehachapi and other horse racing at the farm all the time."

Duke continued, "They've cleared the track, which is a gigantic exception, to allow you to work Tehachapi on the main course.  There will be several other outriders to get you if you are in trouble.  Ignore them."

Duke, Tehachapi and Nina were walking slowly toward the front course at Hollywood Park.  Horsemen were out of their barns to judge the spectacle.

"Pure nonsense," said a respected trainer.

"We need all the gimmicks we can get to save racing," said another.

There was a line on both sides of the shed-row as Tehachapi walked to the main track. No nine-year-old ever rode any horse on the front or back track at Hollywood Park.  Nina would have her tenth birthday in a few days. This being the absolute best birthday present possible.

Riding exceptions made to allow fourteen or fifteen-year-olds to get their galloping license. Nonetheless, it was unheard of for anyone this young—to be considered.

"Take Tehachapi to the gate. Just walk him in as you do at home. Talk to him and get him settled. When the gate opens, give him one whack with a stick, and click off twenty-four-second quarters," Duke instructed.

This was nothing new to Nina. She merely nodded.

"How far? How fast?"

Tehachapi thought, "I can answer the question about the speed of the work before Duke even answers. I knew he would want us to work at least a mile and gallop out. I was anxious to see how the track at Hollywood Park differed from our new practice facility at Cummings Valley Ranch.

"Work him, a mile and a sixteenth, and let him run down the stretch. Gallop him out another half. Obviously, if he becomes tired, pull up. The track here might be deeper than ours at home."

Nina looked directly into Uncle Duke's eyes, with tears saying, "Thanks."

Nina brought Tehachapi on to the main track, and backtracked him away, along the backside at Hollywood Park. Nina used her own judgment in tracking the colt.

"I'm warm," I told her. "I'm floating."

"A little further."

"You're going to kill me before the work," I joked with her.

"Quiet probie."

She turned the tiny, little fellow around when she reached the kitchen, and slowly made her way around to the starting gate.

The gates were situated on the front side of the track, near the far end.

Just as Tehachapi and Nina reached the gates, the announcer said over the Hollywood Park loudspeaker system, "Your attention please, nine-year-old, Nina Torres, will be working stake's winning Tehachapi from the starting gate. Nina is the youngest rider ever permitted to mount a horse in an official work."

The announcer concluded, "Nina has applied for a galloping license here at Hollywood Park, and this will be her official test, as well."

Duke had ridden his pony horse over to the front side, near the wire. That way, he would have a straight view when the gates sprung open.

He wanted an accurate timing; for he believed the time would make people's eyes bulge out. No weight had been added to the saddle. With Nina up, Tehachapi was carrying a feather.

Nina guided Tehachapi without event into the gate. Three boys stood ready to help – none were needed.

"Okay boy, here we travel into history," Nina encouraged.

"Get fastened on, because I'm going to sprout wings," Tehachapi warned.

"Nice and easy. We're going a distance of ground today, so let's have something for our finish," Nina urged.

The starter questioned, "Are you tied on?"

"Waiting on you, sir."

The bell rang and off raced Tehachapi. Nina did not hit him with a whip. She knew he was quick into stride. Nina also realized Tehachapi was never going to be the fastest sprinter – so why try.

Nina rose in her saddle as Angela had instructed her. To any observer, there was grace. To the most critical observer, they might focus on Nina's brace. To horsemen, exercise riders or jockeys, they would only see her balance and her precision.

The trek was underway. To recorders of history, Tehachapi floated above the ground like his father, No Rain. Tehachapi was slightly smaller – although five or six inches longer – than champion No Rain. Moreover, there was an unearthly parallel in their movements.

Duke smiled broadly, as Nina raced across the finish line the first time. He wondered whether the nearly ten-year-old would realize the track was one-mile long – from the wire and back to the wire. Since Tehachapi had started down the track in the starting gates, it was practically a quarter of a mile to the wire.

"Let's see whether she works a mile and a sixteenth or a mile and a quarter," Duke thought.

Duke had told the timer, he was working a mile and a sixteenth.

The announcer said, "Tehachapi's first quarter-mile is 23 seconds."

Duke had the time slightly slower, realizing that it was not quite a quarter-mile from the starting gate to the wire. "That's the difference," he mused.

Tehachapi was one of the most balanced horse racing Duke Snyder had ever seen. Couple his movements with his balance, and Tehachapi worked effortlessly.

"The half in forty-six seconds," said the announcer.

Nina and Tehachapi marched on with hundreds of onlookers cheering. There was nothing uncanny about the two-year-olds speed, until one realized that Tehachapi covered the second half-mile at the same speed as the first.

The nine-year-old worked her pal brilliantly around the course and into the stretch. When Nina reached the pole, which meant Tehachapi had worked a mile and a sixteenth, she came out of her crouch. The child jockey instructed her mount through her reigns; they were galloping out, no longer working.

Duke set times for each eighth of a mile of Tehachapi's journey. He wanted to discern how balanced Nina had reached each pole. To no great surprise, he found the times were the same.

The announcer seemed quite confused by Nina's work, not understanding why she had stood up on Tehachapi when he had worked a mile and a sixteenth. The horsemen and trainers knew. "This nine-year-old could follow instructions."

"Ladies and gentlemen, Tehachapi has just worked a mile and sixteenth in 1:44," said the announcer, once the track's official timer explained what had occurred. Duke had the time faster by nearly a second.

The trainer of one of Tehachapi's main opponents in next year's three-year-old ranks said, "That might seem better than it actually is because she only weighs about sixty pounds. Put a jockey on his back at 115 pounds, and he will slow."

Duke, hearing of the comment, told the Racing Form, "Weight does make a significant difference. Nonetheless, Nina never let him run."

The stewards were impressed with the nine-year-olds performance. They asked to see her handle three more horses the following morning in traffic on the front side.

"Let her get on one of the large No Rainbows colts," instructed the chief steward.

Duke said there was no problem. Nina was up to the challenge. The next morning she donned her helmet, jogging four horses and working two others.

A trainer, who was against someone, so young, holding an exercise license, instructed one of his jockeys to veer in toward Nina.

"Don't hit her – just unnerve her."

"What."

"Stop her," the barn leader said.

The incident was much more dangerous than intended when the older horse actually collided with Nina's mount. That had not been intended, but when you play games, accidents happen.

Nevertheless, Nina maintained her balance as her horse went to its knees. Her lightweight actually allowed her animal to regain his feet without injury.

The stewards were outraged at the antic. They ruled the rider off for 30 days, but were similarly impressed with how the nine-year-old had saved the day.

She was given her provisional exercise license.

"Do not allow her on the course without the trainer being present, and mounted on a pony horse, supervising her efforts."

**Back to the Farm.** In order for Duke's grand plan to work, Tehachapi had to be vanned to Cummings Valley. He was going to race from the farm, which meant he would be taken to Hollywood Park the day before the race.

"I could keep him here. Perhaps, I should let him have his race, and afterward take him back to Cummings Valley," Duke told Angela.

"No. I agree with you. Our life is at our home. Let's make a clean start of it with Tehachapi. Our new life all started with Nina and this little colt," Angela said, giving her husband a long kiss.

Nina, of course, elected to ride with Marty, Mary and Tehachapi back home. She could have flown in the jet, but that would have meant time away from her friend.

The loyal ranch supporters cheered Tehachapi and Nina as they pulled into the barn.

"Tehachapi appears a little thin to me," said Marty.

Mary nodded her agreement.

"I'm going to walk him for half an hour, and I'll start pouring the grub to him before his next race. He's a good eater," she said.

Indeed, I was hungry. I love being back at my home at Cummings Valley Ranch; however, I was not used to the trailer ride, which took something out of me. A day in the sun, even January sun, and some tasty oats would get me on my feet in a hurry.

"Duke was 100 percent correct; I would much prefer my life here at the ranch. Standing in the stall away from home for 23 hours a day seemed similar to a life sentence in prison."

"Agreed," Nina piped in.

"Here, I get out in the paddock, have twice the stall size, and spend more time with friends."

"You better say that."

# Chapter 28

**A New Year's Present.**   Christmas was special that year.  Our ranch was nearly at the 5,000 thousand-foot level, and it snowed occasionally.  Most times the snow would stick around for a few hours, and then rain would wash it away.

"Look at the beauty — all around. God is truly the most fabulous painter."

Snow blanketed our tiny village farm as a quilt hugging a child's bed.  The morning light twinkled off the frozen flakes, attached to the pine trees in the mountains.  The young horses at Cummings Valley played and bucked in the white paddocks.

Nina came to the barn early, and turned the warmblood and me out in our special paddock.  She clogged me playfully with a snowball she made in her small hands.

"Watch it," I joked.  She did not appear to understand me.

There was something different about my girl that morning.  We grew up together, the two of us.  We were strangers from the rest.  Now she collaborates one with some others.

"Today, however, I noticed something new about Nina."

There was no longer an anguished hunch in her back.  Nina stood erect, proud, and happy.  Her crippled leg was stronger now.  Yes, she walked with the slightest of a limp, but only a slight reminiscence of yesteryear.  The long gallops and our artful breezes have strengthened her atrophied muscles.

"She was no longer an ugly duckling – but a pretty swan,"

I said to myself. I spoke to her as I had a thousand times before. Nina looked at me, and I understood for the first time, she heard my language more or less as other humans do.

"More, than less," I said to myself.

Nina and I would always have moments together that would be closer any others. She was now plainly a part of a family, with love and tenderness. As it should be—the love of family was embracing her.

"At first, it broke my heart; then, I realized true happiness for her could be realized only among family."

We were drawn together out of misery. Now, we were being pulled apart by love.

Marty, Mary and Tommy came out to my paddock to visit with Nina and me. Mary hugged Nina, as a mother would embrace a daughter. Marty picked up a snowball and threw it at Tommy.

"I love you, my Nina," I said.

Nina stood frozen in time, looking at me. She said nothing. Then, a smile came on that beautiful face and touched my heart.

I spent most of Christmas Day with the warmblood. An odd friendship developed between us. Some say that people of different races can never blend.

"I doubt that," I told the warmblood. "Look at what good friends we have become."

I was still somewhat slow. There was no way in the world I could race with the fastest thoroughbred across these small fields. As No Rain knew, victory is at the end of the journey – not the start of the quest.

The afternoon turned chilly and cold, when the sun set behind the mountains. The wind whipped over the snow drifted paddocks. Nina came out early and walked me to my heated stall.

A new language was born between us that day. She curried me, and patted me tenderly with love, as she put me away for the evening. The faithful friend, she remembered my blanket – even though there were presents to unwrap with her family.

In the following days and years, I would speak to Nina, and she would absorb what I was telling her. I would hear her words as clearly as yesterday, and love her for them.

**The Days Chilly Stage**. No one needed to tell us that this was winter, because even at noon the Cummings Valley winds blew through us. Our track slowed by freezing temperatures.

"Remember, slower and longer is better," Duke drilled into Nina's young head. Before she would ever mount my back, Nina would say, "slower and longer."

The litany was instilled into her, and would be the formation of her style for decades to come.

Duke and Angela did not believe I needed any additional works. They had Nina gallop me a mile, and take me on a jaunt through Cummings Valley.

"I believe Duke has found a race for you on New Year's Day at Santa Anita," Nina told me. "As I understand it, this will be a small field going at a mile and an eighth. Angela says the competition should be light; so they don't believe you need another work."

I wanted to ask questions; however, without being able to communicate thoroughly with Nina any longer, we had to speak almost telepathically. We had grown up together, and without words, we still could understand one another.

"I imagine you wonder whether I will get to ride you in the race. I asked – believe me. I asked. Uncle Duke says there is no way in hell, they're going to allow a nine-year-old jockey."

I had been hoping we could continue our magic together. I understood rules had to be followed. The racing industry is hurting. There used to be 40 or 50-thousand at Santa Anita on a Saturday afternoon. Now only a handful trickled to the track. Millionaire business-persons are at the tracks; even so, they cannot figure out how to excite patrons.

"We get them out for the Kentucky Derby, and certainly for the Breeders Cup. Many other days are an embarrassment," Duke told Charlie Hinkle, owner of a major stud farm in Kentucky.

"Every-day-Joe believes racing is for the rich. They are not going to come until we get a voice similar to Chick Hearn and the Dodger's Vinny. We need a voice that resonates into the hearts of everyone."

"You're right. The guy who drives the bread truck or the waitress at Denny's must feel a part of our sport before we have a chance," Duke said.

Hinkle magnified the problem, "We can't even get sportscasters or sportswriters to include us in the papers and news accounts every day. We are irrelevant."

The two racing aficionados debated how to turn the Sport of Kings back to its glory days.

Duke said, "We have to stop calling ourselves the Sport of Kings for starters."

"Perhaps, what you did with Nina Torres at the track is one way to climb back into relevance. When a little girl, with a crooked and braced leg, has the guts to climb onto the back of a 1000-pound thoroughbred, that opens minds," Hinkle said.

Duke was proud.

"Nina is something special. So is Tehachapi. When a runt can ride a runt to victory, it makes us all feel as if we have a chance. This little girl has made her own breaks."

The next morning, Charlie Hinkle unbeknownst to Duke called farm owner Tyler Dovato. Just to brainstorm. Tyler was a longtime mentor of the sport, along with his wife Catrina.

"It's going to take something more than a Triple-Crown winner to thrust horse racing back into the forefront of people's minds. We are starving incrementally. In order to keep our sport going, we are going to have to invest billions, unless we can generate public support," Hinkle suggested.

"You're right, of course," Tyler agreed. "What do you have in mind?"

"This Nina Torres girl, who deservedly was granted her exercise rider's license at Hollywood Park, is my first thought. She is young. She is Hispanic – a minority. And she rides with a steel brace."

"I don't understand."

"She is Tehachapi's everyday rider."

"So?"

"We need to convince the stewards at Santa Anita to give Nina her jockey's license," Hinkle pronounced.

"Her license?"

"Absolutely. Not for her – for us."

It was clear that Tyler Dovato, a billionaire and resourceful leader of racing, did not understand where Hinkle was going.

"I'll spell it out for you, Tyler. Racing is in trouble. Nina Torres is the future of racing. Nina and her horse Tehachapi must be entered together. Let mom and pop cheer to see a child's dream come into fruition," said Hinkle.

"Now I understand – brilliant. Did you explore the idea with Duke when you were with him earlier?"

Hinkle said, "No. I wanted to get your intake first."

Tyler Dovato and Charlie Hinkle set up conference calls to more than a hundred people that afternoon. By nightfall, they had a powerful union of support behind the entry.

Hinkle had another three-year-old that was favored in the early going for the Kentucky Derby. He said he would fly his horse to Santa Anita to help make the race news worthy. It will be national news. He told the group that he would welcome any rider who in combination with a horse would make the race a national sweetheart event.

"We need to start thinking about our sport instead of our pocket book," he stated. "I will let America pick my jockey if it makes the race better."

The next morning the stewards at Santa Anita had more than three hundred telephone calls—all supporting the notion that a jockey's license should be issued to Nina Torres. These calls were from national leaders—powerful men and women. Many were not from the horse racing community. They merely supported the concept of helping minorities and children with dreams.

"Mr. Steward," the secretary said, calling over the intercom. "The President is on the line."

The head track honcho had so many calls that morning his usually quiet and friendly demeanor boiled over.

"The President of what?"

"The President of the United States, Sir."

"Oh, I guess I have time to take that call," said the Steward, regaining his sense of humor.

"Mr. President."

"Sir, I know you are busy. I certainly do not want to interfere. Nonetheless, it has come to my attention that a nearly 10-year-old, with a disability, is being considered for a jockey's license," said the President from the Oval Office.

"Yes, sir."

"Respectfully, we should do everything we can to embrace the young. Especially, young people with disabilities, who have exhibited unearthly desires to be great. America is their land. We are people who came from nothing."

"You're right, Mr. President."

"Thank you for taking my call."

With that, the leader of the free world, a racing fan, was gone. To the President, no more vital spokes in the wheel exist than encouragement of the young, the poor, and the disabled.

Hinkle and Tyler Dovato appeared personally before the stewards explaining how critical change was required in the sport. Hinkle had flown all night to be present. A fact, he did not let the stewards overlook.

"Give her a license and the seats will be filled. Newspapers will print stories. TV will give us time. We will be relevant," Hinkle told them.

"She impressed us when she applied for her exercise license. There is no question, she can ride. Furthermore, she has been raised around horse racing," the head steward agreed.

"However, that doesn't mean she is ready to ride in a race at her age," countered the one anti-Duke official, who still had a seat at the power table.

"We need her. Racing needs her."

Tyler said, "Tehachapi is a stake's winner, and she's ridden him her entire life. She's safer on him than anyone. Ask her aunt Angela, whether she would be safe. Angela is a jockey herself, and has trained Nina."

Horse racing is an old boy's sport. That is part of the problem. Change comes hard – if at all. Since horse racing has done something one way for a hundred years, the authorities believe it should be done that way for the next one hundred.

"We won't be here in twenty years, unless we start doing things differently," said Hinkle, who himself had been raised around racing. "Breeding horse racings is all I know. My dad, his dad bred racing stock. If we don't bring new blood from the general population into a racing we are cooked."

The debate went on for thirteen long hours. It was almost as bad as trying to work out a new salary agreement for the NFL or the NBA. The stewards and the establishment said "no" on one side, and the owner's group said, "We must do it now," on the other.

"Get the hell out," said the bellicose steward at one point, ending the meeting.

Within thirty minutes, a call from the governor's office reinstated the negotiations. You see, the governor received a call from the President as well.

Even with the governor's support, old-school racing did not go easily. In the end, the ground swell of support for little Nina Torres and Tehachapi was too much for the Board of Governors and stewards to overcome.

Nina Torres became the youngest jockey in America, with an apprentice license.

A day later Tehachapi was entered in the one mile and an eighth stake's race for New Year's Day. Unlike normal racing events, which drew no column inches in the newspapers, Nina Torres and Tehachapi made front-page headlines in the LA Times and across America.

**"9-year-old to ride at Santa Anita."** One headline read.

This was a banner headline, front page, in the Los Angeles Times. Similarly, the New York Times and other publications shouted the news. There were features on evening radio and television.

Charlie Hinkle's three-year-old Hinkle flew out from Aqueduct to challenge Tehachapi.

"We are at some disadvantage making the trip at the last minute, but since I was an advocate of allowing Nina Torres to ride, I felt we must support her. I am hopeful Hinkle can run away from her and win the event. In any case, it will start a chase to the roses that will not be forgotten," the breeder said.

What we predicted as an easy race was now shaping up with 11 starters. Everyone wanted to be in on the good time.

Nina and I shipped to Santa Anita the night before the race. There was tremendous excitement at the farm when we left.

"Go get them, the warmblood told me." If I did not know better, I thought I saw a tear, Tehachapi said.

I felt excited to have my friend Nina as my pilot for the race. I sensed a calm in Nina, which was normally seen in women many years her senior.   Little Nina had gone through so much already in her life that she was well prepared for events like this one. Nothing special compared to having a family.

"Easy as pie," she said with a wink.

# Chapter 29

**The Match Race.** Little did we know the New Year's Day event would create a flashback to decades before – reminding horse goers of the legendary Affirmed and Alydar.

Santa Anita was crystal clear for the race, not a cloud in the sky. The mountains, which create the backdrop for Santa Anita, appeared touchable from the grandstands.

When champion No Rain and No Rainbow had their duels, there was always inclemency surrounding race days, with howling winds and rain. Not today. It was brisk, but visibility was unlimited.

Nina and I went out for a slow jog on the Santa Anita course in the morning. Duke wanted to be certain his niece had the jitters washed off her, and that I knew the course before we started.

Similar to an old pro, Nina had me stand on the outside rail taking in the early morning sun.

"Good-luck today Nina," said exercise-riders as they went past as Tehachapi and Nina stood.

Duke also lifted her up on two other mounts to ride that morning. Both horses, Nina had ridden at the farm, so she knew them well.

I was more excited that day – by far – than Nina. I wanted to have my little princess in the saddle. Later in the afternoon, Mr. Brown led me over into the inspection barn, where my lip turned outward and my tattoo inspected.

"I don't know what they thought they were going to find. There wasn't a smaller colt at Santa Anita, so who else would I be. Stop with the lip reading, already," I said.

They, of course, said nothing.

Mr. Brown was so old that his bones creaked. You could hear every movement he made. His steps were practiced ones, taken with intelligence.

"Just another day in the park," Brownie said to me. His calmness uplifting.

Other grooms were clearly agitated. Their charges were taking in the electricity and becoming wound up. Not so—with Brownie and me. After doing the pre-race chores, Mr. Brown sat on an overturned pale with his head drooped and fell asleep.

Mr. Brown would die at Hollywood Park later this year, having spent a lifetime in racing. When he died, there was not a dry eye in our barn. I cried for him, as did the humans. He had no family away from the track, so Duke and Angela paid for his funeral—attended by hundreds. He did so much for so many great horses dating back to Hall of Fame trainer Charlie Wittingham. What he did for me that day—a racing instinct of calm, confident peace. And Love.

"You come on, now – works to be done," he said with a wink.

The groom behind yelled at him, "Pick it up old man, or I will run you over."

"Pass if you want. We have one speed – slow. However, it is steady," said Mr. Brown. No words were truer.

I might start the race like a poke, but I was still poking along at the end of the race at the same pace. When you add the entire poke together, it was faster than many champions raced.

Mr. Brown led me over to the saddling enclosure where Scrap and Duke met us. Their grooms in the pre-race barn riled many of the horses up. So, they were jumping around like a cat on a hot tin roof. I sat motionless while Duke fixed my racing saddle.

"Let's go get your Nina," Duke said to me, understanding I was anxious to see her.

We walked out of the enclosure, up to a path, which led into a large circular fenced area, where the owners and jockeys met the horses.

It was quite spectacular to see my Nina walk confidently, brace and all—out with the other jockeys to meet their horses.

"Oh, she's so small," I thought.

Others were saying the same thing. Fingers pointed, and astonishment registered on the faces of men and women alike.

"Maybe, they will miss my size today," I conjectured. "But probably not."

We would later find out that 67,520 people attended the races. Every seat taken in the grandstands. People were elbow to elbow near the saddling fence.

This was history. Nina was America's sweetheart. For that matter, New Year's Day racing was America's sport.

"Nina, we've gone over it... Get Tehachapi away. Don't get stuck. I want him to go a quarter in twenty-three seconds. That is not fast for him. I want him up at the front of the pack in a good spot," Duke instructed for the umpteenth time.

"Uncle Duke, I've got it. Find a good position, keep him going at a forward pace, and run them off of their feet."

"Right."

"I understand none of them can go as far as Tehachapi. I also understand all of them are faster. I am going to be certain that none of them have anything left. Slow pokes at the end of the race," Nina smiled.

The Great Race Place was great again. There seemed to be a million voices. Every seat a smiling faced. People were standing. Many had to watch the races from television monitors because there was no place to view the actual oval.

We were all warmed up, backtracked and all. Nina snaked her way to the starting gate. Nina and I had drawn position nine, and our main challenger Hinkle inside us in gate four.

Duke Snyder and Angela had started their relationship with Duke watching the races on the television set under the grandstand, so other owners would not disturb him. As their love grew, Duke and Angela found a place in the turf club where they watched it at a solitary table.

Here today, Duke had found his old position watching the stake race where he first had seen his beloved No Rain fly from the heavens to defeat No Rainbows.

No Rain had a slightly different running style. He had an amazing turn of foot, and could combine it with his legendary ability not to tire. No matter how far he raced.

"That is somewhat dissimilar to me. I don't have any of Rain's finishing lick; perhaps, I am imbued with even more abilities to run a route of ground."

"The flag is up," the announcer broadcast.

The betting public made both Hinkle and me the prohibitive favorites.

Hinkle proved to be much faster – similar to No Rainbows. He was able to take the early lead. Nonetheless, Duke's instructions were followed to the letter, and Nina directed me from the starting gate briskly and with a purpose.

The eastern invader was in no hurry after gaining the early advantage; however, was setting a brisk pace. Around the first turn, Hinkle had us by a length. I was third on the outside floating along.

"We are clicking off quarters in twenty-three today boy," Nina instructed. She was developing a stopwatch in her head.

"Track feels good, smooth going," I replied.

Onto the backside, we raced with Hinkle holding the clear advantage early. Through the half-mile, I raced in 45 2/5, and was now tracking second.

The next quarter went along just as fast. Nina pushed the button, and put me on even terms with Hinkle. She did not want too much to do in the stretch.

"We've raced six furlongs," said the announcer. "The pace is a breathtaking – 1.09."

Never before had three-year-olds going this distance raced as fast. The pace for Hinkle was one he had handled winning a six furlongs race earlier in his career. However, now he needed to go a mile and an eighth.

The race already boiled down to only the two of us. The others were far behind. Plodding along.

Duke said, "Nina is pushing the pace at Hinkle. I know Tehachapi can keep going – we'll see about the easterner."

We were racing around the turn, with Hinkle on the rail. I did not understand it, but when I ran at Hollywood Park or Santa Anita, I seem to have more oxygen in my lungs than even in the mountains. Nina had tried to explain something about, there was more air at sea level – whatever that meant.

"All I know, this is living."

We flew into the stretch.  Hinkle was giving me a mad glare, which earlier in my life would have scared me.  No more.  This was not a sprint.  I had my Nina, now.

"Down the stretch – they are head-and-head," yelled the announcer.  "Mighty Hinkle on the inside, and little Tehachapi trying to keep up on the outside," the announcer barked.

Nina made an experienced riders move by guiding Tehachapi slightly inward toward the rail crowding Hinkle.  She was not so close that anyone could disqualify her.   Clearly, however, she was crowding on the large thoroughbred.

For the experienced horsemen, viewing the duel, it was a great move.  Little Tehachapi threatening a horse eight inches taller.

There was no separating the horses.   They were eyeball to eyeball.   Only to the discerned eye could understand the jockey aboard Hinkle was whipping his mount--on handed, because Nina was too close for jockey hand maneuvers on Tehachapi's side of the racetrack.

Nina sat motionless.

She did not ask the Little Giant to run yet.

When the horses were six strides from the wire, Nina flipped her reigns at Tehachapi.  That everyone saw.

It was "my single to fly."  I waited for my orders from Nina, and for my head.  And here it was.

"Now it's Tehachapi inching away, coming to the wire a head – or perhaps, a neck in front."

The announcer was the one out of breath, unable to speak.

The battle down the stretch renewed a rivalry long past.

"Both horses have eclipsed the track record," reported the announcer. Neither quelled anticipation of when they would meet next – similar to heavyweight champion boxing.

Charlie Hinkle said, "That was one phenomenal ride by Nina Torres. I didn't appreciate that she crowded my champion, but you have to admire her intelligence in doing so."

Hinkle lost that day; nevertheless, it renewed keen interest in the sport. "The greatest minute or so in sports," reporters wrote.

In the winner's circle, Duke threw down the gauntlet, "No clear winner emerged today. This may be the most exciting time in history leading up to the Kentucky Derby. When will Tehachapi meet Hinkle again? Will Nina Torres be permitted to ride in the Derby?"

Finally, trainers were starting to promote the sport. Tehachapi and Hinkle both had run faster than any before at Santa Anita. Faster than all the great ones.

Will Hinkle run in the Santa Anita Derby? The television and radio special reports throughout the country questioned when the two great horses would tangle again.

**Back at the Barn.** Everyone wanted to know how much more Tehachapi had in the tank at the end of the race.

"You guys were moving," said Angela. "Did you know you had enough for the end of the race?"

Nina answered, "We raced evenly – at one pace throughout. I did not ask him to run until the very end. Normally, I would have let him run an eighth of a mile. Hinkle is special. I could see he was not tiring much either. So, I saved a little extra for the finish."

"Brilliant," thought her aunt.

Duke asked, "Is that about as fast as Tehachapi can run in his floating style?"

"Nope.  Didn't really push the button. He can make a mile and a quarter or a mile and a half at the same pace.  What is more, for the Santa Anita, I will let him run an eighth of a mile down the stretch," she told the trainer.

He winked.

# Chapter 30

**Hinkle Taken Home.** Sportsmen Charlie Hinkle announced he was flying his great three-year-old, Hinkle, home to Aqueduct to run in the East.

"I owe it to the people to run my star there. He started his campaign in New York, and the fans should be able to watch him grow up. Our plans, barring injury, would be to take him to Kentucky for the Derby. Perhaps, if little Nina Torres and Tehachapi make it to Kentucky, there will be a rematch."

Duke Snyder said it was premature to predict where any horse might run on a given day.

"Injuries dictate so much of what we do. I admire Charlie Hinkle for flying his great horse to the West Coast on a minute's notice. It would be legendary if the two superstars of racing get a chance to race again. Clearly, nothing has been settled this early."

Similar to Charlie Hinkle taking his horse home, Tehachapi was vanned in a brand-new Cummings Valley Ranch box car to his home in the mountains. No small trailer for this colt. The truck painted brightly, proclaiming the ranch name and the saying "the home of No Rain and his son Tehachapi." Riding in the cab of the truck happily was Nina Torres, America's darling.

Time at Cummings Valley ranch was exciting. Breeding season was underway with great expectation now that No Rain restored to prominence.

Likewise, Duke had begun training more of the Rain progeny to run extended paths, understanding that they were one-paced horses. "Go long young man." Duke would say the slogan – over and over. Angela, it is a play on words, taking its history from "Go West young man," informed Nina.

"He's such a goof," Nina told everyone.

"You are right about that. Even so, I love my goof," Angela proclaimed.

Catrina and Tyler Dovato lamented that they had given up on their champion, No Rain. On the other hand, the friendship between the Dovatos and the Snyder's was as strong as ever. The Dovatos had many Rain sons and daughters who started to prosper at the races.

Despite the words to the press about racing in the Kentucky Derby, Duke and Angela counted backwards from the first Saturday in May. Another milestone in the step to Kentucky is the Santa Anita Derby, scheduled the first week of April.

Duke computed that Tehachapi could easily run once more prior to the main Santa Anita attraction.

Telegrams or voice messages arrived, inviting Tehachapi East to the Wood Memorial and other prominent races for three-year-olds.

"There are two schools of thought," Duke said. "We can stay here in the cozy confines of California, and sweep the western events without risking injury. Alternatively, we can go East and challenge Hinkle on his own course, prior to the Derby."

Angela, thought for a minute, and responded, "I believe we should do whatever proves your theory that we can run off of our ranch."

Two other winners were trucked to Santa Anita from the farm—returning to the ranch after winning in Arcadia.

"Certainly, three winners aren't much of a legend; however, I don't see much difference between shipping a horse from Hollywood Park to run at Santa Anita than vanning from here. It amounts to thirty extra minutes in the new box car. It's similar to shipping in from Hollywood to Del Mar."

Mary, who predominantly shipped distances with show horses for jumping events, queried, "To me, the primary difference to compare is the quality of the tracks the horses prepare over. Is Hollywood Park safer than working in animal here?"

"Most horsemen would unequivocally say yes. Hollywood Park and the major tracks have more resources to prepare the tracks."

Duke went on, "However, I believe our training surface here is more uniform. We judge it minute-to-minute. If Marty determines something needs doing, we stop and adjust. There hundreds horses work on a major venue, and the tracks become rutty and uneven."

Angela added, "I believe another factor is altitude. If we prepare horses here, and run them at a lower elevation they have more endurance."

Marty added, "Yes, it's like when the Lakers go to Denver and struggle with their legs, because they're playing at a higher elevation."

"There is nothing in the rule book, which prohibits a trainer from preparing a horse at five thousand feet, and then running him at sea level," Duke explained.

The group continued their conversation throughout the days as they prepared younger horses for their racing careers, and brought additional horses from the track to the farm to continue the experiment.

"One thing is for sure, for us to execute fully – running off Cummings Valley Ranch – we are going to need more stalls," Duke concluded. "When we are at Hollywood Park, if we need ten or twenty extra stalls, we go to the barn manager and request them. Not so easy here. We are limited by stalls available."

Duke and Angela were in their nesting period as they waited for their baby. Nina and Tommy joined Marty and Mary back at Mary's warmblood farm. Therefore, Duke and Angela felt lonely without the children's chatter.

Instead of moping, they used the kitchen table, and both drew plans for the revamped Cummings Valley horse ranch.

Angela concentrated on planning beauty for the facility, including drawing areas for ponds, fountains and flowers.

Duke worked on the practical. His vision included mare barns for the expectant moms, a small but somewhat lavish stallion barn to hold four stallions, and an expanded racing facility.

The racing stock has more practical needs—traditional stalls and ceilings. The existing giant edifice used for breaking and training young horses.

"I think we should discuss extending our half-mile track," said Duke.

Angela countered, "Why don't you leave it as is, and prepare a new mile one. The smaller oval is perfect for starting young horses. The mile oval used for works. I know it would cost more initially, but in the long run I believe we would have fewer injuries."

Duke agreed. He immediately started planning where the mile track. Fortuitously, Duke and Angela had a hundred and sixty acres, so there was more than enough room.

# Chapter 31

**A Marriage Holding Separate Dreams.** Angela fitted herself seamlessly into Duke's well-orchestrated life. When they met, Duke was already an established horse trainer. He had worked tirelessly in that endeavor, and it was clear Duke possessed innate talents with racing stock.

Angela grew up with horses, and excelled as a show-jumping star at a young age. By the time her father died, Angela was jumping in Grand Prixs with riders more experienced and older. However, even there Angela won her share.

She gave up the dream, because without her father's financial input, she could not buy the expensive horses required to continue competing.

Angela moved to the track, and into stark stable quarters, in order to continue her passion with horses. There she found another passion – Duke. She fell head over heels for him.

Angela excelled as an exercise rider and groom, because of her affinity for the animals. She had a rare talent as a rider. She instinctively knew what horses were going to do. This skill allowed Angela to find the perfect takeoff spot for show jumping, and the instinct allowed her to be an instructive pilot for racing stock.

Together, Duke and Angela were a loving combination that brought tranquility and expertise to the mountain ranch.

January 8th, Nina had her 10th birthday. The fanfare included a small party in front of Tehachapi's stall, where Nina blew out 10 candles atop her birthday cake. Angela had offered a bigger party, but Nina wanted Tehachapi involved.

February was warm this year in the mountains. The horses, including Tehachapi excelled.

Nina at 10-years-old was growing mature for her age. The bond at Mary's warmblood farm shown on the children's faces. The adult's, as well. Warmth and love for humans are akin to light and water for plants. Nourishment.

On a mid-week night, Angela and Duke were walking together from the barn to their home. They were dawdling – pointing at where their dreams were being built. They were dreaming as kids do. Walking as lovers.

Duke already started construction on a sixty stall racing barn.

Angela carved out acreage for her ponds. Duke said they were as big as lakes.

"Going to call this lake, Michigan?" he quipped.

Duke paused.

"What other dreams do you have, my love?" Duke asked.

This is the first time Duke ever inquired, or for that matter, considered Angela might have dreams that differed from his.

He was immersed in expanding his training opportunities; he did not encircle her visions. The first step back was when Duke sold off his eastern racing barns, and set on a path for training at home.

"You hit one of my dreams with a Bull's-eye," she said giving him a hug. "I had always dreamt of living on a horse farm, and working with horses. Cummings Valley Ranch is bigger than I imagined."

Duke, feeling there was more, asked, "What else?  What else is included in your perfect dream?"

Angela stopped, taking both of Duke's hands.  She looked up into his loving eyes.  Angela understood why horses performed so well for him – he was tender, caring, and compassionate.

"You are," Angela said, with tears in her eyes.  "You and I form a family.  I pray God will give us some healthy children, who can enjoy the blessings of this farm.  It is clear to me the footprint of love is planted deep here."

Duke asked, squeezing her hands, "What else for you?  You are so giving; you place your needs behind mine."

"I guess, I saw myself as an Olympic equestrian, and performing in the Olympics as a show jumper," she confessed.

The tears were coming now.  Full-blown.  Angela had never told anyone – not even her father – that she hoped to jump the big fences in the Olympics.

Duke followed Angela on a pony horse the first time he saw her ride.

As she rose in the saddle, Duke saw beauty and something special.  Angela helped Tehachapi's mother become a race filly.  His mother never wanted to be a horse racing.  With Angela's kind heart, Ms. Mary relished the task.

Duke, nevertheless, had never seen his Angela take a jump over a fence.  He knew she had been a show jumper.  Yet, he had never asked her to jump.

"Why?" he wondered.  It was as if he had been whipped; Duke was ashamed.

"I'm sorry.  I am so sorry," said Duke.  Tears now came to his eyes as well.

"No, you shouldn't be sorry.  How could you know?  I never told you."

"I love you so completely, Angela.  I should have known.  I want to see you jump.    You said you were a show jumper.   Why didn't I ask?"

The two grabbed each other, clawing and kissing – tongue-to-tongue, love-to-love.  Duke fell on one knee, and Angela was soon on the other.  They necked like teenagers.

"I think we need to rearrange some of our thoughts.  I don't have any experience in what's needed for a show jumping facility," Duke said.

"Clear to me the big arena in the barn would be ideal for your sport."

Angela said, "We don't have to do that."

"Yes, we do."

Over the next week, Angela - with Mary's help - figured what was essential to merge a show jumping dream in the otherwise singular horse racing farm.

Duke was fortunate in racing.  He received blessings from Jesus.  More than luck.  Duke blessed with innovative ideas that worked.

"We'll plan our lives here together.  Perhaps, Tehachapi can be the momentum that brings us to both our dreams," he said tenderly.  He kissed her on her nose.

Tehachapi prepared by a series of works for another start as a prelude to the Santa Anita Derby.  Duke was able to find another stake's handicap five weeks before the Santa Anita.

Marty and Nina came to Santa Anita, driving a six-horse van, which was taking Tehachapi and four other starters to the races.  Duke had found five races over two days for the enventors.

"An amazing thing is happening in Tehachapi's race," Marty told his daughter on the bumpy ride.

"What?"

"Only three other horses are challenging Tehachapi in the mile and an eighth contest."

"Why dad?" Nina asked.

"Remember the days when you and Tehachapi hung out together? He asked.

"Sure. Never will forget."

"Everyone thought he was such a loser. Believed he would never make it to the races."

"Right."

"Now, because of his ability to run and run, without tiring, everyone is afraid of him. Three other starters are running because they know they will pick up checks finishing second through fourth," Marty explained.

Nina was busy on this trip to Santa Anita. Duke had her on each of the five horses in the morning. One was a particular challenge. Even though, he was four-years-old and a multiple winner, he had a reputation —he would run off.

"This will be a good experience for you, perhaps in a bad way," Duke explained.

"How's that?"

"You are going to have to figure out how to jog a thousand-pound horse, and not get carried away."

Nina had already learned from harrowing experiences in Cummings Valley that her little arms were no match for any horse, including Tehachapi, if it wanted to run away with her.

The morning was uneventful until Thundering marched on to Santa Anita.  His ears told Nina he was ready to be a rogue. The gelding took two steps. With every sign, he was going to bolt away. Nina put both hands on the right reign and cranked his neck all the way to the right.

"Angela's told me no horse can run off if it's running in circles." She smiled to herself.

The gelding was frustrated and took three large threatening steps. Nina taught astutely by Angela—had great balance and racing intelligence.  There was no way this four-year-old was going to put her on the ground.

"Settle down, you rogue," she said giving him one whack with her stick.

Nina straightened the gelding out to backtrack away again. Thundering still believed he could get the best of her.  He took two more threatening steps with his ears planted.

This time Nina wielding him to the left said, "Better learn your lesson."

Nina gave Thundering, a reassuring pat on his neck. No stick this time. Instead, loving pats.  She him turned around to gallop.

"Here we go, be a good boy."

Angela might dream of going over six-foot fences in some far-off land in the Olympic Games, but she also thrilled at seeing her husband and niece win five straight races over two days.

"My hubby knows where to place horses, so they can win. Nina braved the inside at the rail to win the first, and took one wide becoming victorious in another.  Both good decisions." Angela crowed to any who would listen.

Joe Calamos did not like the days Nina was at the track. He lost winners.

Tehachapi and Nina were unbeatable. A tall gelding with Duke's everyday rider Calamos in the saddle tried to put it to them. Joe had the gelding sprint away, going twenty-one seconds for the first quarter, and following it up with a blistering twenty-two seconds for the stanza.

Nina told her friend, "Let him go. We are going to run our race."

"We did run our race today, Nina and me. We were four and one-half lengths behind Calamos after the first quarter mile and about the same after half-mile. The difference was we kept up our pace."

Calamos and his gelding fell out of the race. They jogged around finishing fifty-seven lengths behind us in the end. We continued our fractions all the way to the end.

Nina let me run the final eighth of a mile, and jog out a rapid half-mile beyond the wire.

"Ladies and gentlemen, Tehachapi has won in a track record time, by sixteen lengths. Bring on all comers for the Santa Anita Derby in a month," announced the track spokesperson over the loudspeakers.

"No one could say Nina had a weight break as Tehachapi — the little runt — actually carried the most weight. "

Added weight packed into the saddle.

Duke telephoned the ranch to gloat with Angela, who had stayed at home on the farm, but watch over television.

"The most impressive thing about the race is that Nina brought home Tehachapi faster the final quarter than in his first. Both your little star and my turf warrior are growing up together."

Angela asked, "No Rain was a terror in the stretch.    Is Tehachapi starting to pick up his daddy's tricks?"

"Could be."

# Chapter 32

**Contention in the Santa Anita?**  Track officials were sweating over the lack of contenders for the Santa Anita Derby.

Tehachapi had run over the local crop.  Who would want to face this three-year-old who broke a track record every time he stepped on the course?

Santa Anita was the beneficiary every time Nina Torres rode. She had started in races on three cards, and each time, there were more than sixty thousand people in attendance.

The Great Race Place was back.  Advertisements told spectators to buy their tickets early.  No one could have conceived of having to pre-buy race tickets.  When she did not ride, many days you could not even give them away.

Santa Anita announced one week after Tehachapi's track record race that the Derby was sold out of turf, box and reserve seats.  The track officials were fighting with fire marshals figuring out how to crowd more than a hundred thousand patrons in for the Santa Anita.

### Kentucky a Different Story.

"Are you guys crazy?"  Duke asked.

The Kentucky Derby ran in a different jurisdiction than either Santa Anita or Hollywood Park.   The officials in Kentucky announced they were not going to allow a ten-year-old to jockey on any horse within the state.

"Kentucky is tradition.  We are horse racing.  Maybe a gimmick works in California; we have real horseman and jockeys here," the czars of racing announced.

It was early for the Derby. No one knew who would compete. Nonetheless, Tehachapi in the West and Hinkle in the East were the prohibitive favorites.

Commentators speculated, "Kentucky sees itself as a predominantly eastern powerhouse state. They believe if they can force Duke Snyder to pick another rider for Tehachapi it will take the little horse off his game."

Angela counseled Duke to be patient.

"You normally don't get ahead of yourself. You still have to win the Santa Anita, and that is a one million-dollar race. Winning that race alone will prove you are right about training at the farm, and pay the bills here for a year."

"You are right. It just pisses me off."

"Language," she said, slapping him on the rear.

"Watch the hands, lady?"

Duke's percentage of wins soared, with more and more winners running from Cummings Valley. The farm christened the sixty-stall racing barn. Duke employed revolutionary concepts to keep the barn warmer on cold nights and cooler during the hot summer months.

To Duke's credit, three more sons of No Rain won stake's races, all running from the ranch. One was a gelding that Angela had purchased from a disgruntled owner for $2,500. He won in a gallop, going a route of ground.

"Our share of the purse pays for a hunk of the new barn," Angela said with glee.

As Angela's pregnancy progressed, Duke started insisting Angela stay off horses. Spend more time coaching Nina and the other young 15-year-old rider. We are not taking a chance with our family," Duke told her.

She did not want to take time off, but she knew the risks. Her butt was toast more than once, hitting the ground.

So Cummings Valley was a place of change that early spring. Construction, hope for the Santa Anita Derby, for their yet unborn baby, and for the future.

Nina and Tehachapi were relegated to long gallops.

"Nothing better," agreed Nina.

"Perfecto," Tehachapi's retort.

Duke saw no reason to work Tehachapi. He was in good flesh. He didn't need to go faster. He needed to remain sound.

Since Angela was grounded, Mary and Angela worked putting the final touches on the show jumping designs. The big barn used as a combination facility, housing horse racings on one side and jumping horses on the other. Likewise, the arena would have a dual purpose.

"Look at this jump?" said Angela. Mary, Nina and Angela were busy on an early evening picking out the Grand Prix jumps. The colorful jumps to be placed in the new arena, which was built between the large barn and the front road—the country street in front of Cummings Valley ranch that brought visitors to the farm.

The facility would seat 3,500 hundred spectators, and was large enough to put on a variety of shows, jumping events, including a mega Grand Prix.

"Our farm now looks like a show jumping haven from the road," teased Duke. "Marty, don't you think the girls are trying to run us off?"

"Sure looks like it. Flowers, streams, ponds and white fences are what you see from the road. Oh yes, and those large jumps," Marty said.

In fact, it was Duke's idea to put show jumping in the front, which would leave him room for two tracks, and his barns in the rear. Angela knew, but loved him for what he had done, once he recognized her dream.

Duke continued to campaign for Nina. He offered to fly her to Kentucky, so she could try out for the track officials.

"Normally, one state accepts the license from another state. Jockeys from California do not have to audition for the stewards of another locale," Duke complained. "But we will campaign in this instance."

Coming up to the Santa Anita Derby, most trainers worried whether their horse was good enough. They worried their horse might go too fast, or take a bad step. In the run-up for this Santa Anita, the main issue was Nina Torres.

A week before the Santa Anita, there were only four sure entries for the big race. Duke had two horses owned by Catrina and Tyler Dovato that would be good enough most years.

"Catrina, do you want to challenge Tehachapi? Or, run elsewhere."

Catrina said, "Maybe we can have another one, two, and three finish in the Kentucky Derby."

In the end, Catrina and Tyler gave their blessing. One contender shipped in from Florida, because the owner and trainer believed the track suited him, and he would do no worse than second.

Scrap called Duke saying, "Nine will go in the Santa Anita."

"With all the money we are spending here on Cummings Valley, we can use a big payday. It is good for racing that there are nine. I understand Hinkle will only face five other starters in the Wood Memorial," Duke said.

Odd's makers still believed Tehachapi and Hinkle were the odds-on favorites to win at Churchill.

"Scrap, have three stalls ready tomorrow," the trainer said. "We will bring Tehachapi a couple of days early to be sure everything is settled before the Santa Anita."

Scrap said, "It is quieter at the ranch. You are not going to get any rest around here. Furthermore, we are going to need a guard to keep the crowds away from Tehachapi."

"A guard is a good idea. Set it up."

# Chapter 33

**Dirty Tricks for the Santa Anita?** The press wanted to know whether Joe Calamos was going to try any filthy, under-handed, tricks in the big race. Calamos was disappointed at losing mounts to Nina, and especially not named to ride Tehachapi.

"First, I'm on a contender in the Santa Anita; second, trying to run a horse and a rookie jockey off their feet is smart not dirty tricks; and third, certainly, everyone's going to be looking for an advantage. With Tehachapi, you have to do something to stop him from running even fractions all the way around," said Calamos in an interview to the Racing Form.

The national press, Las Vegas, and the betting public had all decided Tehachapi, barring injury, would slip away to another earthshaking victory in the Santa Anita Derby. The track tried to drum up competitive interest in the race. No one took it seriously.

As amazing as it was, every advance seat sold for a race; for which the public already knew the outcome. This the first time there were no seats available in more than three decades.

A TV commentator said, "It might be the most watched rerun in history."

Duke had enforced a media blackout at Cummings Valley Ranch, where dozens of news trucks had dotted the lane in front of the farm. He did not want Nina stressed by having to respond. Her teachers also agreed to have a watchful eye.

"Pressure, what pressure?" said the girl who was once listless without human friends. "It's all unreal."

However, now they were at Santa Anita; Nina was fair game. The media had press badges, which allowed them access to most of the Park. Trainers, for the most part, could keep those vultures at bay within their individual stables.

Nina still walked with a slight limp. Her brace was modified to a slimmer, but stronger metal, which would protect her leg. The ten-year-old simply ignored the fuss.

Her life was Tehachapi, her family, and horses.

She considered the interviews tiring. The first one she did was intriguing; however, after that she saw the questioners as boring. They got in the way of what she enjoyed.

"Please, leave me alone," she told a CBS horse racing expert. "Go, interview some other rider."

In the morning, the day after their arrival, Nina told Tehachapi, "Come on. Let's get away from these creeps."

The groom lowered Tehachapi's webbing, unintentionally allowing him freedom. When Nina gave the instruction, no one was holding the colt. Tehachapi merely started following the ten-year-old, nuzzling up to her.

"Look, she's on the move," said the TVG commentator.

"It's truly unreal how hooked Tehachapi is on little Nina," reported a trainer turned commentator for the horse betting channel.

The beasts, as Nina Torres called them, were all aghast at what was taking place. The star of the races was walking away "no saddle-no halter" – as one expert reported it.

At the end of the barn, Nina grabbed onto Tehachapi's mane and lofted herself aboard.

"Unbelievable," reported the commentator. "I'm not sure what to make of this."

Photographers recorded the incident. It appeared Tehachapi actually lowered his front legs. In doing so, it made it possible for Nina to scurry onto the back of the three-year-old colt.

What was for certain, Tehachapi and Nina were jaunting away without a halter, reins or saddle. Nina showed good judgment by not taking the colt to the front track, but merely walking him to the recesses of Santa Anita.

"Is this little-girl safe?" asked one national, investigative reporter, who made his living on Channel 2 Los Angeles knocking everything and everybody. If there was not a story, he made one up. If there was one, he exaggerated it out of all proportions.

The event captured national media attention and took the overall discussion at Santa Anita. The stewards questioned Duke and Nina why she should not be suspended for the irresponsible act.

"What does 'irresponsible' mean, as you are using the word?" Nina questioned sincerely.

The steward shook with anger when asked. One television camera attended the hearing—to be fed to all the media.

"Irresponsible means rash, reckless, or ill-considered actions," he said simply.

"I didn't show any lack of care in my behavior or that of my stallion," Nina replied. "My intentions were formed from a lifetime of being with Tehachapi. Not once – never – has he acted in an unreliable or untrustworthy way. I do not believe my actions were lighthearted. Not immature. Not dangerous, as some of the TV personalities have stated."

Duke smiled. "So much maturity. Absolute candor. The television writers are searching the Thesaurus for a word that adequately explains the word integrity."

Nina, with sincerity, continued, "There are rogues in the barns here that are not safe with the toughest jockey. Nevertheless, no one says a word when those runoffs endanger the public. Are out-of-control. Not one person has testified or could state that Tehachapi created any havoc. This is all a publicity stunt. A TV show — created by the media – not by me."

The steward asked Duke, "Didn't he believe her actions were hasty; that she breached the moral obligation of jockeys in general to protect everyone at Santa Anita?"

"As far as I know, there is no formal rule prohibiting a jockey from riding a horse in that manner. Certainly, there are many intending to maintain order and safety. The question is – did Nina's actions impair the public safety?"

"Yes – that's it?"

"The answer is no. She did not. If you would prefer, we would submit to a test – Nina will ride Tehachapi wherever directed without a saddle and without reins. Then, the world can judge – you as the final arbiters can rule whether her actions were irresponsible," Duke suggested.

"You're saying Nina can ride Tehachapi safely anywhere on the backside or track at Santa Anita under those conditions?"

"Absolutely."

It was now three o'clock, and the races were underway. The stewards decided Nina should mount Tehachapi in the barn without the aid of reins or saddle.

"Walk him from the barn, to the track, and ride him once around the track."

The vengeful steward, who had a grievance with Duke dating back years before to an investigation of a dangerous drug cartel, made the ride more perilous by adding conditions.

"The brat must complete the ride within two minutes."

"Two minutes." Duke asked, "When does the time start? Does she have two minutes to complete one lap from the time she enters the track? Alternatively, is it two minutes from the time she passes the wire, until she reaches it again?"

The chief steward, who had always befriended Duke, said to the offending steward, "Let's not have name calling."

"I still want it done in two minutes from the wire to the wire."

The challenge had been set. Tehachapi had been out on the track earlier in the morning. He galloped around the oval easily.

Duke had not planned anything else for him until race time. Taking Tehachapi out in the afternoon, and asking him to gallop a mile was something that no trainer would relish. Nonetheless, Nina's youth created an unusual spectacle.

"The glee of that one steward is too much for me," said an honest TVG reporter. "This 'test' is lunacy — not her ride this morning."

The stewards and management of Santa Anita racetrack knew Nina's and Tehachapi's appearance on the track the day before the Derby was sure to be greeted by race goers with delight and merriment.

The news reported as program-interrupters and on sports stations. The rumblings drove people to the track. Businessmen took an afternoon off to view the spectacular. The gaiety added drama and exhilaration to Santa Anita.

"Good for racing," said the belligerent steward.

"What if she gets severely injured?" asked the news commentator.

"Her fault — not mine."

"She's 10-years-old – how old are you?"

"We're responsible for the safety of the patrons at the track."

The media surrounded Duke after the stewards' meeting. Does the ride of Tehachapi 24 hours before the Santa Anita Derby imperil the horse's chances in the championship race?

"Yes. Forcing a horse to route hours before a stake's race does compromise his best performance," Duke replied.

"Do you feel you were treated unfairly by the stewards?"

"No. I believe Nina's youthfulness called safety into question. I spoke truthfully to the overseers saying Nina was safe; however, they acted appropriately by challenging my conclusion."

"What if she falls off?"

"She won't."

"There will be screaming. More noise than you can imagine."

"So what?"

"You don't think Tehachapi could spook? Run off? Nina fall on her crippled leg?

"Nope."

Prior to the stake's race, Nina again mounted her trusted companion. This time assistant trainer Scrap hoisted aboard her. The giant of a man put his hand softly on Nina's leg.

"Go, as easy as silk, girl. Picture the two of you playing in Cummings Valley."

"Tehachapi is such a goof, a show off," exclaimed Nina, "He will prance. He will think it cool."

"Not too much delight.  He will race tomorrow."

"He'll be fine — better than terrific."

### Tehachapi and Nina Front and Center,
### Friday, Santa Anita

Newsmen and the league of the thousand cameras trailed as a line of ants from Duke's stable to the track.

"Ignore them," urged Nina.

"That's an impossibility," I told my girl.  The sounds of the camera operators firing their cameras created a song: "click, click, click, flash, click, click, click."

"You hold on girl," I said to my passenger.  "Take a good hold of my mane."

She said nothing.

"Some 50, 000-plus screamers watching in the stands," Tehachapi reasoned.

She said nothing.

"Lean on me, girl."

I knew Nina heard me instinctively. Not so much my words any longer. However, I had talked to her for so long that it would never end for me.  Candidly, this opportunity for her to ride me bareback was a thrill.  It brought back memories. It was nothing new to us.

Click, click goes the cameras," I sang aloud to myself.

"Why are you singing, Tehachapi?" Nina asked in surprise. She heard me when I was singing. I would sing more in the future.

"Love this." I told her.

Almost immediately, my girl started singing softly a church song.

**"Lead me, guide me, walk**

**beside me.**

**Help me find the way.**

**Teach me all that I must do.**
**To live with him someday."**

My Nina had sung the church hymn a million times, as we chased rainbows in the valley. We did walk with Angels, and I—the too small, creaky youngster — learned the meaning of God.

"Faith." I said.

"That's right. Faith. That we can live with God some day — together."

"They have horses in heavens?"

"You've asked that a million times before, dummy. Yes, of course, God loves all animals as I love you. There are horses in heaven."

In earlier times, Nina's right leg was extremely weak. She would have to compensate by digging her left knee into my flanks, and leaning slightly off center.

Even now, for the most accomplished rider galloping a thoroughbred a mile without a saddle in two minutes around a track was a rigorous task. No reigns – no saddle. Do it in front of 50,000 spectators – perhaps impossible for a young lass?

When Nina explained to me what we were to do, I truly understood the significance.

"They are hoping you will fall," I told her.

"Only one crotchety, grumpy old man hopes we crumble."

"Weird. We won't."

"You're going to have to float—be a butterfly for me Tehachapi," Nina urged. "Get in a rhythm all the way around."

The best thing about that afternoon was that my Nina could hear me – at least for the moment.

Nina was quiet as she sat frostily on my back, as we left the old Santa Anita barn, which had been painted green a million times over the years.

Her new brace dug into my flank on the right side. I would never complain, because I knew how important, this test was for my little companion. However, without stirrups, she had to plant her legs into my flanks.

"Walk," she instructed as we traversed onto the Santa Anita course.

"Right."

"They didn't say we had to gallop until we reached the starting post at the wire," Nina said patting my neck with her left hand.

"Be certain I'm warmed up a little."

She did not appear to hear me.

We walked limberly down toward the rail. It seemed all of Southern California was present at the races, as thousands screamed.

"Nina, Nina, Nina, they called." All the admiration for her. I was very proud. No one uttered my name. They were in love with my Nina – just as I am.

As we approached the finish line for the first time, Nina gave me a knowledgeable little tug on my mane with her right hand.

She gave me a friendly slap on my tush with her left, as she rose like a ballerina, holding on for life with her tiny knees and legs.

I was waiting for clues from my heroine. How would we do our symphony? For, I had no idea how fast we should go.

She was humming a distinctive sequence of notes:

> **"Lead me, guide me, walk beside me.**
> **Help me find the way."**

Her pace gave me the perception of how swiftly to romp. If I started to go too fast, she slowed her rhythm.

**"Teach me all that I must do**
**To live with him someday."**

She slowed and spaced her words, until I returned to the rhythm.

We fell into a step and continuity. Indeed, I practiced floating with soft intervals of landing on the manicured Santa Anita track, and bounding away.

I did not worry about time, because Nina's voice was the cadence, I followed. Before I knew it, we were in the backstretch. I might be little, but I was taking huge strides.

"You're doing great Tehachapi," said the director of the symphony.

We were turning into the stretch, and I was expecting Nina to give permission to proceed to run a little. She always encouraged me the final eighth of a mile.

Today, however, she said, "Be an Angel all the way to the wire – nice, smooth easy strides."

So, I continued floating all four feet off the ground at times, and touching only for an instant, before we went skyward again.

"Easy as pie," I roared.

We passed the finish line for the second time. I felt her joy for an instant as Nina took both hands off my mane. Saw her give an impassioned wave to the throngs.

The chorus coming from the stands was incomprehensible to explain – a thunderous ovation. Shortly, she had her little hands wrapped around my neck.

"Trot," she said.

Shortly thereafter, she pulled me to a walk; headed me toward the barn.

"Once more around," I pleaded.

"You are a clown," she giggled — slapping me on my rump.

The track announcer explained to the crowd that the stewards mandated Nina and Tehachapi to make the one-mile trek in two minutes or less.

"Ladies and gentlemen, the time for one-mile, with no saddle and no reins, was accomplished in 1:42," he nearly screamed.

"Tehachapi with Nina Torres up will compete in the $1 million Santa Anita Derby tomorrow right here at Santa Anita. For now, that is a new track record for someone traveling the distance holding on with her knees, hands, and a prayer."

"Duke, was that too fast? Is it going to compromise his chances for tomorrow?" A reporter asked.

"We will have to see. Remember, Nina weighs only sixty-three pounds. It was much as if Tehachapi doing it on his own," the trainer replied. "He wasn't carrying weight in the saddle."

"Are you worried?" Screamed another reporter.

"Did you see the majesty of his steps down the stretch?"

### Saturday, Santa Anita!

The debate went on overnight. How much had Tehachapi lost, by traveling a mile that fast, 24 hours before the championship race?

A trackman, who was responsible for perfecting the suitability of the course, said he measured Tehachapi's stride down the stretch. He could do it since no other animal had left a mark since it was tilled.

"From the point where he touched, and sprang away with all four feet off the ground to where he touched again, it measured 29-plus feet," he said.

Other trainers and knowledgeable horsemen said that was impossible.

"No one argues – Tehachapi has a long stride. However, even Secretariat couldn't do that."

Some contended that Secretariat's stride reached 25 feet, while others contended that Man-Of-War was the greatest thoroughbred with a reach of 28 feet.

"How could a little runt fly 29 feet — going slow?"

"Impossible."

"Come," said the trackman. "I'll show you."

"No time for such trivia," said the angry steward. He did not want to praise them; he wanted to bury them.

Duke was asked how it was possible for such a little horse to have such an immense stride.

"Some horses gain speed through power; others akin to Secretariat do it through a combination of size and balance; Tehachapi is cat-like," the trainer said. "No one ever measured No Rain's flight. It also was beyond reason."

Whatever the explanation, Tehachapi was led to the post as the six to five favorite. Odd's makers explained that the little horse's maneuvers the day before had given other horses a fighting chance.

"Here we go, champ," urged Nina, as the bell sounded.

For the first time in Tehachapi's racing life, Nina held me off the pace of the three front-runners. It was not that I was going slowly. Arguably, it was because the front-runners were going too fast.

Tehachapi found a nice even pace in a reasonable time about a length and a half behind the three Santa Anita Derby contenders that slugged away at the lead. They were sprinting.

"Bide your time," said Nina, this time with her tiny feet planted perfectly in the stirrups, her back straight as an arrow.

"I don't know what yesterday did, but I'm not taking any chances."

"No confidence," I responded — not missing a beat. "We're flying with the Angels."

She did not hear me.

At the quarter pole, Nina gave Tehachapi her traditional little movement with her hands. To the unobservant, she did not flinch at all.

To me, she gave the instructions to make up the distance. Now.

In reality, Tehachapi was not tired at all. The romp yesterday afternoon was a pleasure; because it broke up the boredom of being in the stall. The three front-runners had been going at it, and separated by no more than a neck.

"Here comes Tehachapi," screamed the announcer. The crowd responded with a roar. Nina is letting him roll."

Like the mighty champion No Rain, Tehachapi sprang on his competition as a cat on a mouse. Perhaps, in the early days this one had no speed. However, after running a mile, Tehachapi wasn't tired at all. The other contenders were struggling for air and stamina.

Into the stretch, I moved effortlessly to the outside of the other contenders, and floated. In one call of the announcer, the others were done — finished — co-put. Over-and-out!

"It's now Tehachapi by two lengths," said the announcer. "It is over. He is making mince-meat of the competition."

There was no new track record that Saturday afternoon, but little Tehachapi had shown everyone his ability to eat dirt and close from behind.

After passing the horses, Nina gave the slightest of a movement with her fingers, which told Tehachapi to gear down his charge.

Past the wire, the duo floated on for another three-quarter of a mile.

"Tired," says who.

"You goof."

She could still hear my words at times. More when we were together and alone. When she was with Mary and Marty—not so much.

# Chapter 34

**The Great Debate.** Following his win in the Santa Anita, Tehachapi reclaimed his paddock with Angela's warmblood as his companion.

"Welcome home," bellowed the warmblood, towering from above me.

"You appear to have grown another foot tall in my absence," I told him.

"No. Just my pride showing. I got to jump over some of the big jumps. Only knocked one down."

"Why did you hit one?"

"Angela. She took off too far out."

"Likely story."

"Any way, we—the jumpers—now have taken over. It's a mutiny. We have the front of the ranch. You racers get the back of the bus," said the warmblood. Prejudice is everywhere – even with horses, and, of course, with other animals.

"Who pays the bills here? We do. Duke says I just made 550-thousand clams. Don't know why clams are important," Tehachapi said.

"Me neither. How's Nina."

"I'm still in love." Reported Tehachapi.

The fervor of westerners was heard worldwide, trying to force Kentucky to give little Nina Torres a riding license. Enable her to mount Tehachapi in the Kentucky Derby – a provisional license for one race.

Kentuckians, nonetheless, held firm that a 10-year-old should not be permitted on an American racetrack, let alone in America's greatest race.

"And a 10-year-old girl, after all," cried a Kentucky sports show. "I still don't think we should spend money on girl sports, at all."

Only days after winning the Santa Anita, Duke received an official overnight letter, which stated unequivocally he would have to obtain the services of another jockey. A new rider should he want to enter Tehachapi in the Kentucky Derby.

"Ten-year-olds don't have a place being jockeys. Should be playing dolls. They are too tender in years to appreciate the immediate choices a rider must make. Juvenile behavior will lead to havoc. Not in Kentucky," said the letter in part.

Duke released the letter to the media, including a statement.

"The decision of the Kentucky stewards is an attempt to tilt the tide toward Hinkle. I consider it unfair advantage to take Tehachapi's everyday rider away from him in America's biggest race.

"I openly admit that Hinkle was at a disadvantage when the horses met here in California," Duke continued. "He flew in without adequate preparation. Now, it is time for America's best turf stars to meet without handicap."

Upon hearing Duke's comments to the press, the Kentucky stewards went ballistic. In fairness to them, Duke's statement was taken out of context—and exaggerated.

In any case, the stewards unanimously suspended Duke Snyder from racing any horse, anywhere for 60 days.

In a statement released to the press, the head steward said, "Mr. Snyder can apply for a rescission of our order if he apologizes for his comments and selects another rider for Tehachapi in the Derby."

Duke flew from the ranch into Los Angeles International Airport. He drove to an urgent meeting with the stewards at Santa Anita. His question was simple. Were the stewards in California going to uphold the ruling by the Kentucky authorities?

"If so, I'm out of business. Nina and Tehachapi are shut down."

He did not notify the press of his meeting with the local headmasters, wanting to minimize the acrimony towards them. In the hastily assembled meeting, Duke presented his exact words; he had recorded them.

By a two to one vote, the stewards ruled, "Duke Snyder is not banned from racing in California."

The order published to the media. The official words, "We would have preferred him to have chosen a different tone when he complained about losing his rider. However, we do not find that Duke Snyder has committed any violation of California racing."

Staying overnight, at his Marina del Rey apartment, Duke Snyder telephoned the stewards at both Maryland and New York to find out whether he and Tehachapi were banned from their races. The second and third leg to the triple crown.

Ordinarily, a disqualification from racing in one jurisdiction carries the same holding in all.

"We hope you can resolve your difficulties with the Kentucky stewards, so we do not have to differentiate between the rulings in Kentucky and California," he was told by the Maryland authorities.

The second rung of the Triple Crown held there after the run for the roses in Kentucky.

The Aqueduct stewards—where the third leg ran annually, said, "We certainly hope that Tehachapi and Hinkle both compete. We welcome Nina Torres and will grant her a license. You are not suspended here."

No Rain was the first horse to win the Triple Crown in more than 35 years. Duke and all the participants at Cummings Valley Ranch hoped his son could duplicate the feat.

"What do you think, Angela?"

"If you don't apologize to the stewards you are going to have a lifetime of trouble with them," she said. "Is it worth it?"

"No."

"Then?"

Even though Duke had won permission to race in California, the next morning, he wrote a simple letter, which he would send overnight and release to the press.

"I apologize for the remarks I made, which were inappropriate. Furthermore, I accept that Nina Torres will not ride races in Kentucky. I understand I will need to appoint another jockey to race in your jurisdiction," he wrote.

Duke waited, without further comment, for three days. Finally, the stewards in Kentucky announced, "The disqualification of Duke Snyder to race in Kentucky has been reduced. He will not be allowed to race here through the Kentucky Oaks day, but will be allowed to train here for the Kentucky Derby and enter for America's premiere race."

It was still a severe penalty because the ranch had two outstanding three-year-old fillies. They were bared from the Oaks.

The press descended upon Duke the following morning asking, "Who will ride Tehachapi in the Derby?"

Everyone speculated the ride would fall to everyday rider Joe Calamos.

However, Calamos said, "I have not been released from my agreement to ride for Catrina and Tyler in the Kentucky Derby."

Their horse finished second to Tehachapi.

"I still believe if we can find an easier pace, we have a hell of a chance to beat that damn little horse," said Calamos.

He still was stinging from Duke taking him off the horse in the first place.

Duke refused to say who would ride.

Ten days after winning the Santa Anita Derby, Duke shipped Tehachapi back to Santa Anita early in the morning. He had connected with Calamos' agent and secured permission to work the colt over the turf course.

Duke arrived at Santa Anita at nine a.m., and walked the colt until Calamos arrived at ten o'clock.

Joe Calamos warmed Tehachapi under the instructions Duke had given. He took him onto the Santa Anita turf course, where he worked him a half-mile in 46 2/5, galloping out.

"He moves so similar to his father," said Joe. "I believe, if anything, his stride is even longer. One thing is for certain, he floats over the turf course. I always told you No Rain could have been an exquisite star on turf."

"You certainly did. I remember."

"But why?"

"Why what?" asked Duke.

"Why are we working him on the turf when the Derby is on dirt?"

Every move the trainer made since Calamos first saw Tehachapi was a mystery to him.

Duke had the confirmation he was looking for. The trainer observed every foot of the work with binoculars. Also employed the horse racing network's videographer to tape the turf move.

Calamos' agent said, "Do you have permission for him to ride Tehachapi in the Kentucky Derby, and take him off Catrina's horse?"

"Not yet. As I told you, this work was an accommodation — a favor. I wanted Joe's opinion on how he went over the grass," Duke said.

"Why?

"I'm just trying to plan the colt's future."

Finished with the work, Duke walked Tehachapi for an hour and a half.

Duke hummed a few beats of Nina's church song as he meandered, walking his 14-hand horse. He was playing his cards close to his vest. After training hours, he unceremoniously loaded his star into the back of the two-horse trailer and rumbled down the road – headed to the mountains.

### Rumors Start to Circulate.

Within days after the turf work, rumors flowed from England where authorities indicated Duke had pre-entered Tehachapi in the Epson Derby at a mile and a half on the grass.

Rumors also circulated that Tehachapi scheduled for the St. Leger at a mile and six furlongs. These are two out of three of the English Triple Crown races.

Duke continued racing horses locally, but Scrap was always on hand to saddle them. Duke and Angela worked at the farm, with the telephone off. The front gate at Cummings Valley Ranch closed—and locked.

"No admittance."

He had received a telephone call on his cell phone from Catrina, who heard rumors that Calamos might not be available to ride her three-year-old in the Kentucky Derby.

"I assure you Joe will ride for you, as promised. Let's win the Kentucky Derby together."

"What are you doing with Tehachapi?"

Catrina was sharp. She had been around Duke for years and realized you could not assume anything. So, she did not ask him who was riding, but where the horse was running.

"Taking him to England. The rumor is correct. I'm running him in the Epson Derby. I believe a mile and a half will favor him—even more than the Kentucky Derby's length."

"They are going to say you are ducking Hinkle," she prognosticated.

"Not if we can beat him with your horse," Duke laughed.

"Is that possible?"

"Yes, I believe it is. Everyone's going to be gunning for Hinkle, and we are going to be running for the roses."

### Reverberations.

The horse racing community was dismayed with Tehachapi's withdrawal from America's biggest race. Everyone knew, even if some were not saying, Tehachapi was going to England where 10-year-old Nina Torres could ride.

"You are not ducking Hinkle? You're sticking with Nina, even if it means going to England?" The Los Angeles Times horse racing writer conjectured.

"Right. Going to England." Duke's response.

The Santa Anita race course single-handedly was saved from financial ruin by the interest the fans had in the young rider. Even the supporters of Hinkle could not bring themselves to say Duke Snyder was dodging their horse.

"It's Nina," said Hinkle's owner. "Duke is as loyal a man as there is on the planet. Only Nina will ever ride Tehachapi."

Churchill Downs officials downplayed the decampment of Tehachapi.

"This is perhaps the strongest field in the history of our race."

The statement was untrue, but made to save face. The answer came on a bitterly cold Saturday in May when only 52,000 spectators showed, instead of the more than 185,000 who were expected. Even those present said they were disappointed and depressed by Tehachapi's absence.

The race itself was anti-climactic. Ten other entrants sprinted away surrounding Hinkle. The horses went stride for stride with a large reddish chestnut, impeding his progress.

"They've boxed him in. He has nowhere to run," cried the announcer looking at Hinkle's predicament.

In the stretch, all the combatants except Hinkle folded, but the crowding of the favorite had taken its toll. Calamos made a desperate run with Duke Snyder's trainee.

"It's Hinkle by one length, Paso Robles catching the leader with every stride," called the announcer.

The horses had a sixteenth of a mile to go, and it appeared the No Rainbows' colt, Paso Robles, would go right on by Hinkle. However, Hinkle, the stature and size of Secretariat, responded like a champion winning with heart.

"Now it's Hinkle and Paso Robles head-and-head. They are fighting down the stretch reminiscence of Paso Robles' father," yelled the excited announcer.

In the end, Hinkle persevered by a neck over the Catrina and Tyler Dovato colt.

"Hinkle is one tough combatant," said Duke. "Paso Robles ran his eyeballs out. He showed he is a world-class animal, but today Hinkle was the best."

The commentators asked the question that was on everyone's mind. "Do you think Tehachapi would have defeated Hinkle today?"

"That is unfair. This is Hinkle's day. We'll leave the match race for another course on some future card," Duke replied.

Kentucky missed little Nina Torres that wet and windy day in May. The head steward of Kentucky racing walked near Duke following the race. Seeing him, the man looked solemnly at the ground.

Saying nothing. After all, what could be said?

# Chapter 35

**Across the Pond.** Tehachapi shipped with Angela, Marty Torres and Mary to prepare for the nearly 250-year-old historic Epson Derby. Nina stayed behind because she had to finish her school year; she would leave for England with Duke as soon as school was out.

Europe presented two masterful colts, Sir Henry and The Crown. Both would compete in the race, which was established by Edward Smith Stanley, the twelfth Earl of Derby, in 1780. The race was first run for Stanley and his friends; however, became the world's prestige event.

Such historical names of racing such as Nijinsky, Roberto, and Mill Reef ran to victory in the Epson Derby. Shergar won by a historic 10 lengths in the Epson. After his retirement, he disappeared in the night from Aga Khan's stud farm.

The kidnapping and worldwide search for the champion thoroughbred remains unsolved.

"You are going to be pestered to death," Duke told his niece as they winged their way first-class to England.

Nina looked at her uncle quizzically.

"I know it's easy to say to treat this as another race, but that's what you and Tehachapi must do."

Nina asked, "What do you think the difference will be in this race than in California?"

"Historically, English riders set a somewhat slow pace and charge like wild men down the lane. This type of racing favors Tehachapi. He can set a very even but rigorous pace. I suspect you will find yourself on the lead after a half a mile. You will have to judge the speed accurately."

"If they let Tehachapi run on the loose by himself, they are making a big mistake. He won't quit. Tehachapi is growing stronger," Nina replied.

The trainer put his hands behind his head, leaning back.

"I know."

"He's taller, stronger, and freakishly good," Nina said with supreme confidence.

Duke said, "I don't know if anyone will go with him. Do not forget the race is a mile and one-half – not a mile and a quarter. Any horse can tire running that route of ground. Furthermore, turf is softer than dirt – takes more out of him."

Nina was going to be the youngest jockey in history to start in the Epson Derby. Should she win, she would eclipse Lester Piggott, who won at 18-years-old. Piggott rode in the Epson Derby a historic 38 times, winning nine. In all, Lester Piggott won 5,300 races.

There was mixed reaction in Europe about a ten-year-old lass starting in the race, where there was a formal dress code for patrons—and was routinely attended by the Queen.

"Will Tehachapi be knighted when he kicks their butts?" Nina asked joyfully.

Mary and Marty purchased Nina a formal English day dress and hat to be worn, when she was not riding.

Nina had joked about her dad when he tried on his top hat. Marty was always dressed with jeans and a cowboy shirt at the ranch. It was going to be a spectacle seeing him dress formally.

### Race Day England

More than 130,000 spectators came for the spectacle. Bettors established The Crown, owned by the Queen, as the six to five favorite. Sir Henry and Tehachapi both listed at three to one.

"Why is Tehachapi not the favorite?" Angela asked.

Duke explained, "The Crown is undefeated, and has competed successfully with this class, and under these conditions. Bettors wonder whether Tehachapi will favor the soft English grass; question whether he will get stuck in the turf."

"What do you think about the soft grass, uncle?" Nina asked.

"Ask your Aunt."

"Aunt Angela, how about it?"

"We were not permitted to gallop over this course, but we did have many gallops over similar here in England. I would say Tehachapi's style of floating over the grass, and his extraordinary stride gives him an advantage. That's why I was asking why his odds were so high," Angela explained.

Duke said, "I backed the two of you by betting 20,000 pounds."

At the amount, Angela looked up.

"You've done what?"

"I put our money squarely on Tehachapi. We've invested a small fortune coming over here. If I didn't think he will win, I'd stayed at home," Duke explained, almost smugly.

"Going a mile and a half on tall, wet grass he will win, unless Nina falls off."

"Uncle Duke!" Nina yelped, "Don't jinx us."

"I have faith, gal."

Marty asked, "If you win, what will you receive in US dollars?"

"First, you should have said when we win, and the answer is almost $100,000 by the time betting closes."

The easy banter between the Cummings Valley families went on until it was time for Nina to put on her silks, and Duke to saddle Tehachapi. Even then, as they parted on their way to make history, there was an ease about them.

"Just have fun," Duke said, kissing his niece.

Tehachapi was enjoying the festivities, and saddled with ease. As he walked about, he bowed his neck.

"So small,' said a rival trainer.

"Greatness comes in small packages," responded Duke.

Knighted or not, I was eager to renew my love affair with Nina. We met where the jockeys were glued to their mounts. Most of the jockeys took their instructions and legged up, without any love for their animal. Nina, however, gleefully greeted Tehachapi, petting his ears, nose, and rubbing him about his eyes.

"I love you."

"I love you too, Nina," Tehachapi responded.

These days their talking to each other was innate, nonverbal between the two. Nina was hoisted aboard as the throngs cheered.

As in a flashback, a little girl looking at Tehachapi said to her father, "He's so small. How can a pony run with those big horses?"

When the betting public saw Tehachapi, they began to question his ability. Years before bettors made fun of Tehachapi's father, No Rain. Actually, laughed at him. Until he won like a champion.

In the few minutes, Tehachapi was on the track prior to the race, the punters one and all grouped their bets on The Crown and Sir Henry. Not a pound bet on Tehachapi.

Duke and Angela tried to find a quiet place to watch the race, but there were none.

Angela said, "Duke, Tehachapi is now six to one."

"Englishmen are looking at his size – not his heart. Northern Dancer wasn't tall, but he did wonderfully on the turf," Duke replied.

The group went to the post, and was sent on their way.

"Don't make a mistake, little girl," said one jockey, trying to unnerve Nina.

Another rider yelled out, "Get off the turf – you're going to get hurt."

Nina said nothing.

Tehachapi was doing the talking. Nina let him out a notch at the beginning, hoping to get him in the clear.

She knew if the two of them could ride the fields again – like they did in Cummings Valley where they grew up together – the other horses were "going to have to sprout wings" to catch them as Trevor Denman was fond of saying.

Indeed, the little fellow – too slow to play with the big horses in the paddocks at Cummings Valley when he was growing up – did inherit a four-length lead after they had gone half a mile.

"Is she going to fast Duke?" Angela cried aloud.

"I have her in 45 2/5 over a soft, yielding turf course. Everyone will say this is a suicide pace," Duke replied.

"It's just right for Tehachapi," replied Angela.

Nina and Tehachapi marched on, and the other runners fell further behind. The most experienced and famous jockey was sitting on The Crown.

"She's crazy. No one can go that fast and survive," he yelled to a companion.

The Crown was running fourth some thirteen lengths behind Tehachapi. The jockey on Sir Henry was getting busy and starting his run from seventh.

Duke said, "I had Tehachapi in 1:32 for the mile. That is a world record pace. Nina is running them off of their feet."

"Oh my God, I hope she's not going too fast. I pray she won't be embarrassed,' cried Angela again.

"She's fine." Duke patted Angela on her back before she had a heart attack.

"I don't know if I could take that. Winning or losing isn't as important as her not having a broken heart," said her loving aunt.

Duke put his arm around his wife. Normally, Angela tried to stay quiet, because she knew her husband concentrated on every movement of the combatants on the field.

"She's just fine."

Tehachapi and Nina marched on another quarter at the same deadly pace; were now seventeen lengths in front of the second-place horse.

From behind, The Crown and Sir Henry were sent. When Nina was a quarter-mile from home, she moved her reigns with the tell-all signal to her friend, and Tehachapi – who was floating effortlessly over the turf course – swished his tail once and took off for home.

It was the little runt from Cummings Valley that sped away. Tehachapi came home the final quarter of a mile in 23 2/5, eclipsing the world record by three seconds.

"The little invader from California, USA, has crushed his opponents by twenty-one lengths in turf racing history, as 10-year-old Nina Torres raced into the hearts of racing fans around the world," said a reporter.

Sir Henry finished second, with a tiring The Crown finishing third.

"I didn't believe there was any way possible Tehachapi could set those early fractions and continue forward," said the defeated jockey.

Nina said, "I didn't do anything. I just sat there. We could have gone around again. People just don't understand how great Tehachapi is. The longer the race the more they have no chance."

Duke and Angela had a very good day. The purse was 750,000 pounds, plus their winnings at the tote of another 122,000 pounds.

Within hours, Duke and Angela and their entourage were invited to post race parties. A major stud farm inquired about purchasing Tehachapi.

"Ask her!" said Duke, pointing at Nina.

"Buy him. Are you daft?" Asked Nina in an English brogue.

Everyone laughed.

"How about selling us some breeding shares? We'll send a few of our best-suited mares to him when he retires."

"Righto," said Nina. "He would love being a dad to English royalty.

Understanding she was out of her depth, Nina turned negotiations over to her uncle and aunt.

"Okay," said Duke. "We have an agreement. You have five breedings to Tehachapi, and we get to select among the stallions at your farm—five in exchange."

The men shook hands. It gave both sides unique breeding opportunities.

"His greatness," Duke explained to Nina, "Will be determined when your boy goes to stud.

Mary had a thought.

"Nina, would it help if we went to the farm that purchased rights?"

"Oh, Yes."

### Newmarket, England

Two days later, they all visited the stud farm, and breeding operations in rural England. Newmarket in England was the center of breeding for more than 300 years.

"Do you think Tehachapi will be a strong enough to father future greats -- sons and daughters to live on this farm?" Nina asked concerned. The stallions were beyond impressive.

The horse nursery had more than a dozen of the leading sires in Europe with roots back to the great Northern Dancer, Ribot, Prince John, and the world's outstanding sires.

Duke explained, "In America, Mr. Prospector is by far the most desirable breeding line. In the USA, we breed for speed; in Europe, they breed the classic horse racing. Tehachapi runs further on grass than any horse on this farm ever has. Therefore, Nina his offspring will be champions among champions here."

"I'm so happy Mary suggested we come to this incredible nursery," Nina responded.

"Maybe, you'll have a colt named Cummings Valley by him," her dad said.

Duke conducted business buying nine yearlings. All bred to run a classic distance. He was loading his barn for the future. Duke would offer the yearlings to his clients or run them himself, if they did not resell.

Perhaps, the highlight of the trip came on the next Sunday when Mary and Marty were married in a small chapel on the outskirts of Newmarket. Nina was the flower girl, Tommy the best man, and Angela the maid of honor. Everyone dressed up, and Duke loaded the chapel with flowers from a local boutique.

"This is really cool," said Angela to Mary. "I hope you and Marty will be happy forever, and that your new family will make a home for Nina and Tommy."

As the ceremony progressed and the union complete, it was evident that Nina truly had a mother for the first time. Mary went out of her way to be certain Nina was the highlight, and the day was very much about her.

The group came to England as a family in many parts. They went home to Cummings Valley as a family united.

Duke and Angela agreed to provide financing so Mary and Marty, and the children could have their own farm and home adjoining Cummings Valley Ranch. The hope was that the children along with Duke and Angela's children would live in harmony there for generations.

# Chapter 36

**A Clash of Titans.**   The Europeans, including the new partners in of Tehachapi, were surprised when Duke announced the record-setting Epson Derby winner would be shipped to the Belmont in New York to compete in the 1.5-mile Belmont stakes.

The Belmont, although the third leg of the Triple Crown in America, was not held in as much esteem as the St. Leger in England. Furthermore, the Belmont ran on dirt.   The new owners wanted to establish Tehachapi as a grass-turf star.

Duke did not make quick or easy decisions. He explained to his partners the reason for returning to the United States.

"Tehachapi will run in the most prominent key races that are competed at a mile and a quarter or over.  Tehachapi has beaten the best two horses in Europe."

"True."

"Hinkle has royal breeding.  We need to clean his clock.  Set the standard when Tehachapi retires."

"Could be right.  Just don't get beat."

"Sound advice."

The trainer continued, "He has also defeated the Kentucky Derby winner Hinkle; however, people have downgraded our horse's success because Hinkle was shipped at the last second. They say we ducked him in Kentucky. We want everyone to know we are the shipper this time, and we are going to topple the king of the mountain."

Many times new horses that have not competed in either the Kentucky Derby or the Preakness Stakes are normally entered in the Belmont. Trainers deduce the first two legs of the Triple Crown have worn out the primary contenders.

Hinkle won the Kentucky Derby and Preakness. One more victory and he was the winner of the Triple Crown.

"He had some contenders in the Derby, but ran away by seven lengths in the Preakness. Then, you add Epson Derby winner and Santa Anita star Tehachapi to the mix, and other trainers realize this is truly a match race," explained the trainer of Hinkle.

Winning the Triple Crown is a rarity, and turf commentators were critical of Duke's belated entry into the Belmont.

"His horse No Rain won the Triple Crown after nearly 35 years of desperation after Affirmed completed the three horses sweep. He is trying to prevent Hinkle from winning the Triple Crown, so it will keep his stud fees high on No Rain," an angry New York commentator wrote.

"This isn't about stud fees. People criticized us for dodging Hinkle and going to England for the Epson Derby. They were wrong then and they are wrong now," replied an angry Duke Snyder.

He said, "We would be happy to meet Hinkle in a match race to settle, the best three-year-old controversy. Hinkle has only been defeated once – by Tehachapi. Our horse is undefeated. We are offering Hinkle a chance to redeem himself."

The comment by Duke that Hinkle needed a chance to redeem himself set off a forest fire of comments and criticism.

"Hinkle has just won the two best races; what has Tehachapi won in the United States?"

Duke responded, "To us, the Santa Anita Derby is the first leg of the Triple Crown."

That was it. Kentucky went berserk. How could Duke Snyder say the Santa Anita Derby was the first leg and not the Kentucky Derby? In any case, the fiery words of the competitors had a deafening effect on the

Belmont stakes. Many times, 13 or 14 horses go to the post in the million-dollar event. This year, a field of five horses paraded to the post.

There was more criticism of Duke Snyder when he entered Tehachapi, Paso Robles and No More Rain (both owned by Catrina and Tyler Dovato).

Paso Robles had run second in the Kentucky Derby, and shipped to New York bypassing the Preakness Stakes. Duke wanted to space the races and keep his horse sharp.

No More Rain was a three-year-old colt that had been a late developer. Once Duke realized how No Rain's progeny had to be trained, he won a stake event with the colt at a mile and a half on the grass. As a trainer, Duke was doing his best for his clients the Dovatos.

"We are outraged," said the president of Aqueduct, where the Belmont was held. "Without Snyder's two other entries this would be a match race."

Duke replied, "I can't seem to win with the public recently. If I don't enter, I'm a coward. If I do enter, I should have stayed away. If I enter more than one horse, I'm breaking up the continuity of the race.

"My owners, the Dovato's, have agreed I may scratch their two horses, if - in fact - the Belmont is declared by Aqueduct Park to be a match race.    If the Belmont stakes remain the third leg of the American Triple Crown, my owners are going to run their horses."

Aqueduct Park announced the Belmont Stakes was open to competitors, and not a match race.    At the last second, three supplemental entries were allowed.

Asked to predict the outcome of the race, Duke replied, "I will talk about the attributes of my three colts – not the other entries. Tehachapi is a standout.    Paso Robles is an improving colt, who gained nerve and experience in the Kentucky Derby.  No More Rain is another small colt that can run forever."

"You have another girl riding," asked an inexperienced journalist.

"We put another female rider, Nettie, on him; I think he will be charging at the leaders late."

Duke was asked to predict the positions the horses would finish.

"Tehachapi will win and No More Rain will be in the money.  I think Paso Robles will run well, but it could be too far."

Hinkle's contingency again was disturbed.

"Snyder is saying Hinkle will run either second or out of the money."

Duke had a wry smile. "Controversy makes good races.  If we all knew the winner, there would be no racing."

"That is ludicrous." Said Hinkle's trainer.

Nina Torres arrived on the scene late, because Duke and her parents, Mary and Marty, wanted Nina to have a summer at the ranch rather than in New York.

Angela had been kept with Tehachapi. However, Angela engaged a female exercise rider to gallop the colt. Long gallops – unknown to American racing.

"I'm getting big as a house now, so I need to keep my four feet planted firmly on the ground."

"How do you see the Belmont Stakes setting up for you?" asked a commentator of Nina as she walked to mount Tehachapi prior to the stake's race. She arrived in New York the night before.

"Angela says Tehachapi is doing great; he's getting bigger and stronger. And I expect him to win," Nina said.

The Belmont pre-race talk was similar to a heavyweight fight with fisticuffs and histrionics dominating the actual event.

However, the betting public did not confuse the two stars. In the East, Hinkle was a clear-cut favorite. With bettors located in the West, Tehachapi was all the talk.

The announcer told the sold-out Aqueduct fans, "They're all in; they're locked up."

"They're off in the Belmont," he said.

"Hinkle gets out on top; Tehachapi is going right with him," reported the trackman.

Duke and Angela measured Tehachapi before the Belmont Stakes, realizing he had a growth spurt in the last several months. They measured at just fifteen hands – the size of his father. They realized he had grown stronger, as well.

Tehachapi had proven in the Epson Derby he could click off twenty-two-second fractions and reach a mile and a half.

"Nina has no intent on changing the game plan today."

Tehachapi was on the inside of Hinkle on the racetrack, and the game plan for the Kentucky Derby winner was clear. He let Tehachapi, up on the inside, and he hooked him.

"It's Tehachapi on the inside – Hinkle on the outside head-and-head down the backstretch," reported the announcer.

A head-on shot would later be shown to viewers. Hinkle and his jockey were crowding Tehachapi, and pushing Nina and her mount down on the rail. Turnaround from the first race, where Nina crowded Hinkle.

"Mistake guy," said Nina patiently. "You'll make Tehachapi mad, and you won't be in the same postal code at the end."

They clearly wanted to intimidate both the rider and animal. Hinkle weighed hundreds of pounds more than Tehachapi.

The fractions were fast – killer fast. No horse in history had gone that fast that had hopes of finishing a mile and one-half in distance.

"They are even faster than the Epson," said Duke happily.

"Ladies and gentlemen, they've gone six furlongs in one minute eight seconds reported the announcer. It's Tehachapi on the inside – Hinkle on the outside – no one else in the picture."

Duke anticipated an insane pace. He knew Nina and Tehachapi would click off quarter pole after quarter pole as they did in the Epson Derby. He also realized that Hinkle was not going to let Tehachapi getaway.

"They are at the mile marker, Tehachapi's on the inside, Hinkle by a head on the outside," the announcer screamed.

"The mile has been run in 1:29 a new record for that distance, and they have another half-mile to go."

The announcer took a deep breath.

"The pace is impossible, suicidal. Setting it up for something from behind."

Everyone knew calamity was near. There was another half-mile for these two competitors to run eyeball-to-eyeball, and their split times were off the charts.

Hinkle staggered over closer to the rail pushing Tehachapi down on it. Another step and both Tehachapi and Nina would be forced to collide with the barrier.

Nina realized the peril they faced. She decided the time had come to shake the dust off. She shook the reins at Tehachapi, giving her friend a playful tap with the whip on his behind.

"Easy as pie, let's go now," she chirped, repeating something her horse had sung before.

"What," gasped Hinkle's rider. He knew he did not have much horse under him, and realized Hinkle had taken a bad step toward the rail a moment before.

Tehachapi pricked his ears and took off. In two strides, he was away from the danger. Put a length on Hinkle. He was marching to his own beat floating and punching; the Mohammed Ali of turf racing.

Tehachapi did not stop. Hinkle did. Nina floated across the finish line faster than Secretariat. No horse was as fast as Tehachapi and Nina when running long. No sprints for them.

Hinkle faded badly to be fourth. No More Rain and Paso Robles finishing second and third respectfully.

In the winner's circle, Angela helped Nina down. Nina stood in front of Tehachapi, and gave him a kiss on the nose.

"I love you, Nina," Tehachapi told her.

She stood up tall, and looked her friend in the eye. After failing to hear Tehachapi's voice since she had become rooted in a family.

"I hear you Tehachapi. I love you too." She said smiling.

Tehachapi lowered his head into Nina's arms.

"We showed them – two kids too small and slow—all roses today," Nina said smiling.

## THE END